Milicent's Book

Milicent's Book

CHARLOTTE MOORE

CATNIP BOOKS
Published by Catnip Publishing Ltd
14 Greville Street
London EC1N 8SB

This edition first published 2011
1 3 5 7 9 10 8 6 4 2

ISBN 978-1-84647-080-6

Printed in Poland

For my nieces Kate, Helena and Stella,
and with special thanks to Andrea Reece

The Lord of Misrule
January, 1883

My name is Milicent Bella Ludlow and I am an orphan. Perhaps now I've written it down it will begin to feel real.

Orphan. What a lonely word. It sounds like 'forlorn' turned inside out. Do I feel forlorn? I keep testing my heart for fractures, gingerly, as you touch a rotten tooth with the tip of your tongue to find out whether it still hurts. But my heart seems to be quite whole – hard, even. I must pray to have it made softer.

After Papa died, Uncle Ben swept us up, me and my sister Mabel, and took us off to a holiday house in Hastings. It was so close to the sea that on stormy days the salty spray dashed against the windows like gunfire. It was a pity Aunt Barbara wasn't there. She's an artist. She used to go everywhere and do everything, but then she was stricken with a seizure while out sketching on the granite cliffs in Cornwall in a cold east wind. She had to crawl a mile or more for help. She doesn't travel in winter any more. But she would have loved it at Hastings. She adores wild weather, and she's always trying to paint the sea. 'If I could only capture in a picture a wave just as it breaks, I would die happy,' she says.

The seaside house felt empty at first. It was just Mabel and me, Uncle Ben and Creathy – that's Mrs McCreath, who has looked after me ever since I was a baby. I'm fourteen now. Our brother Harry wasn't there; he's at university, in Oxford. Uncle Ben brought his servants with him, but ours stayed behind at Yotes Court. That's our house. But I mustn't forget to tell you about a *very* important member of the household, and that's Bob. Bob is Uncle Ben's dog. He's a black retriever. His coat's unusually thick and curly; it kept him warm all through the nine months of an Arctic winter, when Uncle Ben's ship was wrecked, and now they are both heroes . . . but *that* story will have to wait for another time.

Well, we had only been in Hastings for a day or two when Uncle Ben announced that we needed to have our spirits kept up, so he invited our Leigh Smith cousins to stay; that's Roddy, Willyboy, Lionel, little Bella and even littler Dolly. Their father, Uncle Willy, is Uncle Ben's younger brother. There were five of them in that family – Aunt Barbara, Uncle Ben, Aunt Nanny, who lives in Algiers, in Africa, Uncle Willy and my mama, who died two days before my fifth birthday. Mama's name was Bella. I remember how pleased Papa was when Uncle Willy and his wife, Aunt Jenny, decided to call their baby girl after her.

Uncle Willy and his family live at Crowham Manor, a big farmhouse not far from Hastings. Uncle Willy is a farmer, and he brought everyone over to visit us in two farm carts! Aunt Jenny was disgusted – she likes to do things in style – but Uncle Willy said he needed to buy some supplies in Hastings, so when he'd unloaded the family, who arrived picking bits of straw out of their clothes, he loaded up the carts with seed or corn or whatever it was and trundled back through the deep lanes to Crowham.

Then the seaside house was overflowing. Uncle Ben romped with us all day long. Every teatime he piled the long table with the kinds of sweetmeats we would usually only see at Christmas; there were pretty little china dishes full of violet creams, crystallised plums, Turkish delight, candied orange peel . . . he didn't seem to think it necessary to feed us on anything wholesome, and he didn't notice how dirty the tablecloth became, though Aunt Jenny did.

As usual with Aunt Jenny it was hard to tell whether she was more amused or disapproving. 'Ben,' she said, 'I declare you president of this crazy household, and Mabel is vice-president.'

'And who shall Creathy be?' said I. I never like Creathy to be left out.

Aunt Jenny smiled her tight half-smile. Her skin is stretched so close across the bones of her face, and her large grey eyes are sunk so deep in their sockets that sometimes she looks like a skull, though a rather beautiful skull.

'What shall we call Creathy?' she pondered. 'What do you think of Archbishop of Canterbury?'

'A female archbishop? Aunt Barbara *would* be pleased!' put in Mabel, and everybody laughed. Aunt Barbara thought it unfair that girls could not go to university, so she started a special college for them at Cambridge, called Girton College. She calls it her palace, and the students are her princesses. She thinks that women should be allowed to do everything that men do, even vote in elections. I think

I probably agree, though Aunt Jenny clucks her tongue. Aunt Barbara even said to me, once, that there was no reason why we shouldn't think of God as a female being. I thought about it, but I found I could only imagine God as a man – a man with a thick beard and a jutting brow, like Uncle Ben.

'Well,' said Uncle Ben, when Aunt Jenny named him president. 'I'm honoured, but I'd rather be the Lord of Misrule. Play the piano for us, Jenny-girl. It's time we had a dance.' And Aunt Jenny smiled at being called a girl, and gathered up her black silk skirts with a sound like rushing water. She settled herself on the piano stool, took off the smooth gold bracelets that she always wore and laid them to one side so that they wouldn't jangle, and let her thin fingers scurry over the keys like harvest spiders. Uncle Ben seized Mabel by the waist and twirled her round and Willyboy grabbed me and we stumbled round, and Lionel took little Bella's hands and Roddy scooped up baby Dolly, who wasn't even a year old, and we cavorted round and round the dining-room table until we all collapsed, laughing, in a heap.

But the next day Aunt Jenny took me to the swimming baths, and she had on her disapproving face. 'Really,

Milicent,' she declared. 'Uncle Ben asked us to come here to keep up the spirits of you Ludlow girls, but if anything your spirits want keeping down. I cannot understand you and Mabel. Your dear father has not been gone six weeks' – (Aunt Jenny thought it unlucky to say 'dead') – 'and yet you two seem to be enjoying yourselves thoroughly. Sometimes I wonder if you are really a pair of mermaids! You don't seem quite as if you can be judged by ordinary rules.'

I didn't answer, because I was lowering myself into the water, and admiring the way my blue serge bathing dress billowed out round me like a cuttlefish's bag of ink. But Aunt Jenny didn't seem to need an answer. She lowered herself in beside me and, between splashes, pointed to a large moon-faced clock that overlooked the swimming bath. 'You have your father to thank for that clock,' she announced. 'I felt the want of a clock at the swimming baths but, being nothing like Aunt Barbara, I didn't think anyone would listen to a request from a mere woman. Your Uncle Willy, as you know, never writes a letter, so I asked your dear father to write the letter for me. He did so, and the money for the clock was raised by public subscription. So every time you need to tell the time when you are swimming here, look up and feel grateful to your father. He was always the most helpful of men.'

I have a great deal to remember my father by besides that dull old clock, I thought, but I didn't say so to Aunt Jenny. Instead I said, 'Once, Aunt Barbara sent him seventy-seven broken pens, and he mended them all for her.'

'Seventy-seven? Gracious! How characteristic of them both.'

That night, I thought about what Aunt Jenny had said, and after Mabel and Roddy had fallen asleep I slipped out of my little bed that stood alongside the big one they shared and knelt on the cold floor. I pressed my forehead against the iron bedstead to make it hurt. I was trying to be like a nun, making my body suffer so that I would become better at sorrow. When I lay down to sleep again I told myself that the following day I would not allow myself any pleasure, but would spend the whole day praying, and thinking about Papa.

But in the morning the wind and the waves were wild, and Uncle Ben took me and Willyboy to the beach to jump off the rocks, and Bob dashed in and out of the spray barking at us as we jumped from greater and greater heights, squealing like the seagulls that wheeled over our heads. One great wave reared like a grey stallion and broke right over the rock on which I was climbing, and my silk dress – black, of course, in mourning for Papa – was ruined by the salt water. 'Never mind,' said Uncle Ben. 'I will bear the blame,' and he held out his arms and I jumped into them. With Uncle Ben's strong arms to hold me and his beard tickling my face, how could I find time or space for sorrow?

The Garden of England
January, 1883

While we were at Hastings there was much discussion about where we should live now that we were orphans.

It was the grown-ups who were talking; I wasn't supposed to know. But Willyboy came to me one day with a serious look on his face. 'M-M-Milicent,' he said. 'They're t-t-talking about Yotes. If I were you, I-I-I'd go and listen at the door.' Willyboy has a stammer, which is why he doesn't go to school any more, and it gets worse when he's upset. He was upset now because he'd heard them talking about the idea of us giving up Yotes Court. Yotes is the only home I've ever known, and Willyboy knew how I'd feel about leaving it, because he loves Crowham, where he lives, more than anything else in the world. 'Willyboy sticks to Crowham like a limpet,' says Uncle Ben, 'and will do until he is scraped off.'

'Come with me,' I commanded Willyboy, and I pulled him by the hand. Together we stood outside the drawing-room door, trying not to breathe, almost. We could hear Uncle Ben's voice, and Aunt Jenny's, and Mabel's. Mabel's was high and strained. I knew she was getting angry, so I said a quick prayer in my head: Please God, don't let Mabel say anything foolish.

'I'm twenty-two years old and am quite capable of managing the household,' Mabel was saying. 'I was in charge, more or less, when Papa was alive. How often I heard him say that he didn't know what he'd do without me!'

'My dear,' put in Aunt Jenny, 'an establishment the size of Yotes is hardly necessary, let alone suitable, for two girls on their own. You have seven indoor servants, as well as three gardeners and the groom. Managing such a place will worry you and wear you down.'

'Mabel,' pronounced Uncle Ben, 'you are a child still in mind, if not in body.' I could just imagine the haughty toss of my sister's head at this judgement! I think Uncle Ben would like it better if his nephews and nieces could stay as children for ever. I even think he'd like to be a boy again himself. 'But perhaps, Jenny, she should be allowed to learn from her own mistakes. Let us renew the lease at Yotes for another year, and see how this bold young madam fares.'

I didn't hear Aunt Jenny's reply, because Creathy started calling for me to come and tidy my workbox – which I own I had left in the most disgraceful tangle – and Willyboy and I went away from the drawing-room door as noiselessly as we could; it wasn't till I reached the landing that I could call out, 'Coming, Creathy!' My heart was thumping; it had not occurred to me that I would not stay at Yotes Court for ever. Agitation made me clumsy, and my attempts to disentangle the skeins of embroidering yarn were so feeble that Creathy asked, 'Child, are you ill?'

We returned to Yotes at the end of January, in time to celebrate Harry's twenty-first birthday. Rex, Harry's pointer, and Scray, Mabel's fox terrier, gave us a tumultuous welcome, and I even think my little cat Toots was pleased to see me! Harry brought a group of his Oxford friends with him, and Willyboy came too, on his own. Mabel presided over the festivities in grand style. Uncle Ben was there, and I knew that Mabel was determined to show him how well she could manage. You may think it strange that I didn't ask Mabel straight out about the plans for Yotes, but somehow it seemed safer not to mention it. 'Never trouble trouble till trouble troubles you' – that's what Creathy would say.

I'm at Yotes now, writing this, and as I look out on the park, the grass glittering with frost and the tall trees casting blue shadows on the smooth turf, it seems so safely familiar that I can't quite imagine that it may not always be my home.

I've never told this to anybody, but one day I'd like to be a famous author. I don't see why I shouldn't be. I've always written things down. It's a family habit. We're a letter-writing species. Every day, twice a day, Louisa our parlourmaid brings in the letters on a silver salver. I like to identify the handwriting. Aunt Barbara's loose hand flows all the way across the envelope. Sometimes it's hard to make out the individual letters, because since her seizure her hand has not been steady and the words merge into one another like a line of unravelling knitting. Aunt Nanny's writing is full of curly artistic flourishes. Willyboy's is cramped, blotched and smudged. He writes with his left hand, and smears the ink as he goes. At school they tried to beat the left-handedness out of him. When Uncle Ben found that out, he told Uncle Willy that he must be taken away from school. 'Modern schools are prison houses for the mind as well as the body,' he declared, and Aunt Jenny admitted that Willyboy's stammer had grown worse and worse since he'd gone to school. It got so bad he almost gave up speaking altogether. So he came home, and had his lessons with a kind old tutor, who went out with him watching birds and catching butterflies, which is what Willyboy likes doing best, and let him write with his left hand again, never mind the smudges.

Oh, I do allow my mind to wander, don't I? I was meant to be talking about my writing, not Willyboy. So, to return to where I was, or at least somewhere close. Yes, writing things down is second nature to me. I've kept diaries before, though I must admit they often run out of puff after a few weeks. January must be the best-documented month of the year, by far! I've got notebooks full of poems and scenes from plays and the opening chapters of novels. But now I'm attempting something new; a story for my future self.

In Hastings, it struck me that 1883 could be a turning point in my life. Change is in the air. All my life, I had thought Papa would go on for ever, and then one day he was gone. I had thought my life at Yotes Court would also go on for ever, but now it seems as though that too could vanish in a puff of smoke.

When we got back home to Yotes, I stood on the cold flagstones in the hall, where I've stood so many times before, and I had the strangest sensation, as if the stones were slipping apart under my feet, sliding away from each other to reveal – what? A dark chasm, and me teetering on the brink.

So I'm going to write down everything I think that's important about my life and family as it is now, and when I've finished, I'm going to seal it up and write this date on it: 1st January 1901. Then, and only then, the thirty-two-year-old Milicent Ludlow can make the acquaintance of her former self.

I don't know what she'll be like, the Milicent Ludlow of the future – and I suppose she may not even be Milicent Ludlow by them, but Mrs Somebody Unknown – but for the purposes of this journal I'm going to imagine she's forgotten everything about the scatty, dreamy, untidy girl she once was. So I'll tell her everything I can, and if she ever reads it, perhaps she'll be able to believe that that far-off girl really did exist, here, now, in time and space. Perhaps it will give her something to hold on to.

First I should tell you something about Yotes Court. It's only a house, but I love it. To me it's a living, breathing being – a character with whims and moods all its own. It's a big house, a long box with high chimneys, built of dark-red brick with white surrounds to the tall windows, which gives it a surprised expression, as if its eyes were open wide. All round it there are gardens – flower gardens first, kitchen gardens beyond – and all round the garden is the park, and the park is in turn surrounded by the farm. So everything is held, framed by something else, which is comforting, and right in the middle is little me! I feel guilty when I hear about poor families living in unhealthy crowded places like the East End of London when we have so much room here at Yotes and no one could say we need it all. Well, no one but Mabel! I said to Mabel, why don't we invite some poor families to stay, so that they can enjoy the gardens and the fields and breathe the clean air that's full of the scent of grass and flowers instead of soot, but she only said, 'Milicent, don't be absurd.'

Yotes is in Kent, which is called the Garden of England because the land is so rich and fertile. Our gardens and hothouses produce so much fruit and vegetables that we make fifty pounds a year by selling our surplus. We give a lot away too. Papa made a habit of packing up hampers and sending them to friends or relations, or to our old servants. Mabel says she'll put me in charge of the hampers on my fifteenth birthday, which is quite soon. She says it'll be my responsibility, and I'm glad about that. I'm already planning the springtime hamper I'll send to Aunt Bar, with grapes and cucumbers from the hothouse, eggs from our hens, and bunches of the yellow aconites she loves so much, which she says won't grow in her heavy Sussex soil.

Yotes Court is about two hundred years old. The double front doors open into a large stone hall. You could fit our lodge-keeper's cottage into the hall and still have room to spare. It's as cold as a tomb. In winter there's a great fire blazing, but you can still see the cloudy puffs of your breath as if you were a dragon. Many family pictures hang on the walls. There's one lady in a beautiful pale-green dress with a double rope of pearls hanging round her neck, but her face has been damaged so you can't see whether she was beautiful or not. I asked Papa how her face got that way, but he said, 'My dearest Lilybel, I am sorry, but there are some questions you must not ask.' Opposite her is a man with long dark curls and a narrow moustache; he wears wide pantaloons of what looks like golden-brown velvet, and buckskin boots turned over at the top. He has a long lace collar with pointed ends; he carries a sword, and to tell you the truth I'm secretly a little in love with him. I don't know his name, so I call him Sir Charles.

A door from the hall opens into one of the drawing rooms, which is our dancing room – we all three love dancing, Mabel, Harry and I. My governess, Miss Kahn, plays the piano for us when we dance. Mabel and I can play too, of course, and Mabel and Harry can sing. My own voice is thin and weak, though I can hold a tune, but when Mabel sings people say, 'She could go on the stage,' which always used to shock Papa. This room leads into the little hall, which in turn opens onto the second drawing room. The two drawing rooms are connected by a folding door; when we have a party we open this right up and make one enormous space. In the second drawing room are portfolios of prints and watercolours. Some are by Aunt Bar, Aunt Nanny and my mama; some are by Aunt Jenny and Amy, her beautiful eldest daughter who is married to clever

Doctor Moore and lives in London. Amy paints flowers on dark backgrounds in rich jewel colours; Aunt Bar prefers wild landscapes and skies full of chasing clouds. Mabel and I paint too. It's another family habit. Mabel likes making portraits; she says she can always catch a likeness. No one dares tell her not to boast. The prints are mainly Indian scenes; Papa lived in India for years and years, before he married Mama.

On the opposite side of the hall another door leads to the dining room and servants' offices. The dining room is panelled, but the panels are covered with canvas painted with pretty festoons of flowers and ribbons, and bunches of grapes with birds pecking at them. My best friend Evelyn Stapleton and I believe there must be a secret hiding place somewhere in the panelling so we tap it all over to see if any place sounds hollow, but no luck so far.

Upstairs, though, there's an old cabinet with secret drawers. Papa knew how proud I was when I found out how to press the hidden springs that opened the drawers, so on special days – my birthday, or the anniversary of my christening, or Christmas Eve – he'd hide a little present and a message for me to find. The present would be something like a string of beads, or a flower made of silk, or a sketch he'd done of one of the horses, and the message would say something like 'For a dainty little lady' or 'To the admired Lilybel'. They were meant to be anonymous but of course I knew who they were from! I stored the messages inside my special tortoiseshell box with the purple satin lining. I'm glad I did.

This cabinet is in the State Room, which is the biggest bedroom, at the top of the square staircase that leads up from the little hall. The Queen once slept in this room, when she was Princess Victoria. That was long before we came to Yotes, but I like to press my nose against the window and look out on the view that royal eyes have seen, so to speak! The State Room is another very cold room. The fireplace is wide enough to roast an ox, but the heat seems to vanish up the chimney. The bed is a big four-poster, with coronets carved at the top of each post; you can get in and draw the thick crimson curtains so that hardly a chink of light can be seen and then you feel quite snug. We cousins all used to climb in together and play at being Arabs in a tent, like the ones Aunt Nanny sees in Algiers. One time, our game degenerated into the most tremendous pillow fight – I don't suppose Arabs have pillow fights, but you never know – which only came to an end when I, the littlest, tumbled out and cut my head upon the fender. I didn't cry out, and I tried to hide the cut under my hair, but the blood trickled down and Roddy said she simply had to take me to Creathy because it would be 'rather dreadful if I bled to death'! Of course we were all roundly scolded for such rough play, but inside I glowed with pride because Willyboy told me that I had been brave. 'You know, for a g-g-girl you're n-n-not bad at all,' he told me. Everyone talks about 'poor Willy's stutter', but I've always thought it made him sound extra clever; his voice is so distinctive.

My schoolroom is on the top floor, not counting the attic. It's large and light and airy. Miss Kahn's bedroom is next door, so she uses the schoolroom as a sitting room when the day's work is done. Some of my lessons I share with Evelyn Stapleton, who is the same age as me, and we talk about whether we'd rather be educated this way or if we'd rather go to school. Evelyn thinks that at school the food would be horrid and we'd have to wear ugly clothes, but I think living with a whole gang of girls might be rather fun. And I love learning. I study French and German with Miss Kahn, but I'd like to learn Italian too, and Latin, and even Greek! Sometimes I feel as if I want to learn everything.

Mabel thinks I'm crazy. She couldn't wait to escape from

the schoolroom. I don't believe Mabel ever opens a book, unless it's a play; she loves acting especially if she can take the leading part. But I love books. I run my fingers along the spines of the books in Papa's study, sometimes, and wish that all the knowledge in there could seep up through my fingers and along my arms and into my head that way, because even if I live to be as old as Papa was, I'll never have time to read all the books I want.

So perhaps I would like to go to school. Evelyn and I both like Miss Kahn, though. There's an upright piano in the schoolroom, on which we take our lessons with her. In the evenings I hear her playing and singing German love songs, and though I can't understand all the words I understand enough of the sorrow in them to feel an ache in my heart.

My own bedroom is a corner room, so my windows look out in two directions. When I sit at my dressing table and brush out my silly wispy hair that won't do as it's told, I look down the magnificent avenue of chestnut trees that leads through the park to the road. Mabel doesn't like the avenue. She says the trees' ancient trunks are too bulgy and irregular, like the noses of old drunkards, she points out, rather indelicately. But I love them, and I picture elves and fairies hiding among the twists and bumps. Mabel is too old to imagine such things. I do hope she won't have the trees cut down, now that she's mistress of the house.

When I sit up in my bed I can look out of the other window. I can see the tennis court, of which Mabel and Harry are so fond, and I can just see the end of the fine old holly hedge that separates the flower garden from the kitchen garden. I love the kitchen garden even more than the flower garden. It may sound peculiar to admire rows of onions and the blue crowns of artichokes and the espaliered apple trees knitted together to form living walls round the vegetables, but I do. I love the way things seem to spurt up from the earth, like water from the back of a whale. If ever I have to leave Yotes, wherever I go I'll make a kitchen garden of my own.

Of course every old house must have its ghost, and at Yotes the little hall is haunted. The servants say you can see a cowled figure, which only appears at midnight on the eve of holy days, like All Hallows or Christmas. Just beyond our avenue is a tributary of the Pilgrim's Road, along which troubled souls used to walk to Canterbury for the shriving of their sins, and in our park there's a lake with a little island on it, with the remains of two walls –

all that's left of a medieval monastery. So our ghost could have been a pilgrim who died before he reached Canterbury, or a monk who lost his home when Henry VIII ransacked the monasteries.

I've never seen this ghost, even though twice I've crept downstairs at midnight to try my luck. But something strange did happen to me once. I'd been out for a walk with Creathy – I was about seven years old, I suppose – when I looked up at the window of a bedroom on the first floor, and I pointed and said to Creathy, 'Who's that lady in the Green Room?' I could see her quite plainly. She had a thin face, very pale, and she was wearing what looked like a white nightgown, and her dark hair streamed loose over her shoulders. Creathy looked where I was pointing, then she stared at me and said, 'That's where your mama used to stand.' Then she said, 'There's no one there. Hurry along now or we'll be late for luncheon.' And she fairly dragged me up the front steps, and would say no more about it.

No Valentines
February, 1883

In the garden here at Yotes a silver fir tree used to grow. It was a hundred and twenty-five feet high, and it was said to be the tallest tree in Kent. When I was seven years old it was struck by lightning. The top thirty feet were destroyed altogether. The rest was split down the middle, the beautiful silver-blue plumes scorched and charred. Aunt Barbara made a painting of it. I told you before that all the women in our family like painting and drawing, me included, but Aunt Bar's pictures are the best. They get shown in proper art galleries in London, and people pay a lot of money for them.

As soon as she heard about the lightning, Aunt Bar hurried over from Scalands, her house in Sussex. 'It is a noble ruin,' she said as she sat down to sketch the tree. But in the end the ruin had to come down. 'It was dangerous,' Papa said. He could not bear to think of us playing in the garden, when it might crash down upon our heads at any time. So the silver fir was sawn up and wheeled away in many barrowloads, and the stump grinder came and ground away the stump until there was nothing left of the tree that had been the guardian angel of my childhood, except Aunt Bar's picture and a bundle of twigs that I saved and tied up with a scrap of silver ribbon. I stowed the little bundle away in my tortoiseshell box, the one with the purple satin lining, the place where I keep all my most precious and secret things.

It was so sudden. One day the silver fir was there, the towering pride of our garden, and it was impossible for me to imagine that it could ever not be there. And then in a flash everything changed. I think of my father's death in the same way. He was old – he was eighty-one, so much older than fathers usually are. But he was always *there*, solid and upright and permanent, like the silver fir. They both made me feel safe.

We never considered that Papa would die, Mabel and Harry and I. Well, I don't know if the other two talked about it, but if they did they never shared their fears with me. I've always been very much the baby. Mabel is already a young woman and Harry has just turned twenty-one. This summer he will leave Oxford, and then he, too, will be truly grown up. He wants to train to be an engineer, and build roads and bridges in far-off countries where they don't have such things. Uncle Ben says being an engineer is a fine and manly occupation, but Aunt Jenny says she would never let Willyboy do anything so dangerous.

Early last year Papa went to London to have an operation, and I remember somebody – Aunt Jenny again, I should think – saying, 'You none of you Ludlows seem to understand how ill your father has been,' but I wasn't allowed to see him until the operation was over and done with and he was home again. And then he looked the same as ever to me, straight-backed and smiling, with his hair and whiskers standing out round his face like thistledown. He even went riding, though Dr Hooker told him he shouldn't. 'King Tom's the finest horse I ever owned, and the sweetest tempered,' Papa declared, 'King Tom will look after his old master!' So we set off together, Papa on King Tom who is a big old bay, nearly seventeen hands high, Mabel on Queen Mab, the glossy chestnut mare, and me, a little nervous, on

32

Robin Hood, who was new to us then, and who is black all over except for a white star on his forehead. I was nervous because only a few weeks before, Robin Hood had kicked the dogcart to bits and broken the groom's arm.

Papa was usually so careful with us, making sure we came to no harm. When the rough gypsy hop pickers arrived every September, he wouldn't let Mabel leave the house on her own. When smallpox broke out in London, he wouldn't let Harry go to visit his friends there. Whenever I caught the slightest cold, I was put to bed and had my chest rubbed with liniment and was fed on beef tea and calves' feet jelly. But it was different when it came to horses. Papa was one of those people who seem to have been born in the saddle. When he lived in India he was a major-general in the Indian army and rode through jungles and across deserts, hunting tigers and wild pigs and searching for criminals who had escaped from prison. From our earliest years we three were taught to manage 'spirited beasts', as he called them. He was so proud of Mabel's 'natural seat', of the grace with which she wore her riding habit, of her courage on the hunting field. Mabel and Harry both sail over hedges, ditches and five-barred gates as if they were mounted on Pegasus, and often Mabel is the only woman in at the kill. I try my hardest, and I'm getting braver, but I know I'll never be a natural horsewoman like my sister.

We didn't venture far on that ride with Papa because we didn't want to risk being seen by Dr Hooker, who lives the other side of Mereworth, our nearest village. We just went down to the rectory, where our friends the Stapletons lived. They came running out to see us – Mrs Stapleton, my best friend Evelyn, and little Frank, who is only four and who says the quaintest things.

It was the first time they'd seen Papa since his operation. Mrs Stapleton insisted on sending her manservant up to Yotes ahead of us with bottles of her dandelion wine, which she regards as a universal cure-all. (I tried it once; it was so bitter that I couldn't swallow it. Luckily I was able to spit it out into a vase of flowers without – *I think* – anybody noticing.) Evelyn quickly gathered a posy of the first primroses for Papa to wear in his buttonhole. Little Frank listened solemnly to Papa's answers to his mother's questions about his health, then he turned to me and said, 'If you are ever old and lost, I will look after you.' He is a droll little fellow.

After that, Papa seemed to recover completely and in the months that followed we never worried about him at all.

Perhaps all our worry was taken up with Uncle Ben, who had sailed to the Arctic and failed to return – my goodness, when will I manage to tell you that story? I mustn't forget; it's very important. We carried on much as usual. Mabel seemed to think of nothing but dances and tennis parties and the friends Harry brought home with him from Oxford. Or perhaps I should say, one of those friends in particular. I don't think it's just in my imagination that she singles out a certain Mr Arthur Glover from the rest.

Harry was mostly interested in cricket and shooting and riding his penny-farthing bicycle, with its great big wheel in front and its tiny one behind. And as for me, I spent my time, as usual, daydreaming and building castles in the air. Whenever I can, I climb into the ivy tree. It's a big old oak, but it's so overrun with ivy that it's like sitting on a springy mattress. Creathy doesn't like me to sit there for long, because it's damp – she says – and full of spiders, but I don't know how she knows it's damp because she's never sat in it, and there are spiders in it, to be sure, but I think spiders are interesting creatures – clever and hardworking. So when my lessons are finished I put an apple and a book into the pocket of my pinafore and make my nest in the ivy tree and let my mind travel wherever it pleases.

When the end came, I was away from home. I'd been to Eastbourne with Creathy – people say I have a weak chest, and sea air is meant to do me good. Papa wrote me a letter every day I was away. He wrote to me about all the familiar things; how he decanted a barrel of whisky into bottles, and how he was obliged to sample it even though it was only ten in the morning, and how he was sure the Queen herself at Balmoral didn't have whisky as delectable as this. He told me how Toots, my naughty little cat, had put her inky pawprints all over his writing paper. He told me how he'd mistaken some visitors for burglars because they'd tried to get in through the drawing-room windows, and how they were planning to use the spit that hangs above the kitchen range to roast the meat for Mabel's birthday dinner, just as they would have done in olden times. He said that the bells of Mereworth Church ought to ring out a peal when I returned because everyone was so much looking forward to having me home. His last letter to me he wrote on the morning of 30th November. It was about the arrangements for my return. 'My darling Lilybel,' he wrote – he always called me Lilybel, which was what I used to call myself when I was too young to say 'Milicent' properly – 'I shall take care that the carriage shall be at Tunbridge station in good time to meet the 12.50 train.' The handwriting is exactly the same as always – even, regular, so small that it's hard to read unless you are used to it. No doctor, no scientist, no professor, would be able to examine that letter and say, 'The man who wrote this in the morning will be dead by nightfall'.

I've kept the letter, of course. I'll keep it for ever, in my tortoiseshell box. I took it out today to look at it, because today is St Valentine's Day, and Papa always used to send a Valentine to each of us, and that made me reflect on how I'll never again receive anything in the post from Papa. There were no Valentines for me today. I *think* there was one for Mabel – but that's another story.

'Your father had the kindest of deaths.' That's what Aunt Bar said to me. There was no pain, he would have known nothing about it. His heart simply stopped, like a clock that the servant has forgotten to wind. I can see why Aunt Bar called it a kind death, but I'm not sure I agree. I don't think I would like to be snuffed out like a candle. I think I would like time to prepare myself, say goodbye to people, ask God if he was ready for me. Death is like a journey. It's better to plan.

What gloomy thoughts I'm allowing myself! But it's not

37

surprising that I should think about Death a good deal, since he has already devoured half my family. I began by telling you that I was an orphan, didn't I? My mother died two days before my fifth birthday. And the reason that I am so much the baby of the family is that there was another child, between Harry and me – Edmund, the brother I never knew.

Edmund
February, 1883

The earliest memory I have is of my mother throwing my toys into the fire. A pack of cards – the 'Happy Families' game – and a little Algerian camel given to me by Aunt Nanny. The camel was made of soft brown leather stitched together with thick red thread. He had an embroidered saddlecloth covering his hump. I saw him writhe on the hot embers as if he were alive, and I think I screamed. But it may have been my mother who screamed. A scream runs through my memory like a trail of gunpowder set alight, but where it begins I can't be sure.

My mother's name was Bella, which is also my middle name, though in some ways I wish it wasn't. Bella means 'beauty', which is all wrong for me. When I was born, Aunt Jenny said I was the prettiest baby she'd ever seen. And Creathy never tires of telling me how she took me in my perambulator to a fête which was opened by Princess Alexandra, who of course is married to the Prince of Wales and will be our queen some day. She is generally reckoned to be a beautiful woman. Creathy lifted me out of my perambulator – do you know, I think I can still remember looking up into its big black hood – and held me up to see the pretty lady, and the princess saw me and said, 'What a beautiful little thing!' Well, those were my glory days. I know I'm not pretty now.

Milicent comes from old words for 'work' and 'strong', which I prefer. But Bella was right for Mama; everyone says she was a beauty. I can't properly recall her face. I can see her hands, which were always fidgeting; they were thin, and covered with red scabs and abrasions. I didn't want them to touch me. I remember her thick brown hair, which Hart, her maid, used to arrange in coils pinned on the back of her head. When Mama was unwell, she would pull out the pins and let it tumble down over her shoulders, and once I saw her rub it with ash from the garden bonfire. She streaked her face with mud and stood in the garden looking as if she was about to unbutton her clothes. I was watching from the window of the day nursery. Papa ran out to her. I heard him call, 'Bella – no!' and he threw a cloak round her shoulders. Then Creathy saw me, half-hidden behind the curtain, and she pulled me back into the room.

So, when I hear people say Mama was beautiful, it feels as if they are talking about someone quite different to the person who rubbed ash into her hair, and in a way they are. I think there were two Bella Ludlows. There's a marble bust of the one people prefer to speak of. It stands in Papa's study, serene and graceful, like a goddess. This Bella Ludlow painted the delicate little landscapes that fill the portfolios in the drawing room; this is the Bella who rode out proudly by Papa's side and was considered the finest woman among the hundreds at Lady Brassey's ball. The other Bella Ludlow slashed her bedclothes with her sewing scissors and threw her meals on the floor but ate lumps of coal and wax instead. People think I'm too young to know about these things, but I do know. I have a good memory, and I listen to what the servants say.

Bella means 'beauty', but it also means 'war', in Latin. That's what Harry told me. He studied Latin at school. I would like to know it too, but I never had a governess who could teach Latin. Of course Harry, being a boy, went away to school. Beauty and war – I'm afraid that fits with what I know of my mother. Sometimes it felt as if she was at war with all of us, but really I think the two sides of her nature were at war with each other. I suppose I think of it as her light self and her dark self, a bit like Heaven and – the other place, the opposite; I don't like to write the word.

Do I miss Mama, I wonder? Can you miss someone who died when you were five, and whose face you can't truly remember? I know Papa missed her. On the anniversary of her death, which is 6th March – two days before my birthday – he used to pick a posy of celandines and wood anemones and put it in front of her marble bust in his study. Then he would spend most of the day in there, quiet and alone – alone, that is, except for his thoughts of Mama. He told me that when she was kept in bed after I had been born he used to ride through the lanes and fill his hat with celandines and wood anemones to bring back for her. He said that was the last time Mama was truly happy; he said she was happy because I had arrived. Celandines are so cheerful, opening up on the roadside banks like little new-washed suns. Wood anemones are sometimes called windflowers because they flutter in the wind, like delicate lawn handkerchiefs waving out of carriage windows. They are white with the faintest streak of violet and they look so fragile, but because they bend to the wind it never knocks them down.

I was going to tell you about my brother Edmund, wasn't I? I'll do that now, and get all the sadness over with. Then there'll be no more, or so I hope.

Edmund was born when Mabel was two and Harry was one, and I, of course, didn't exist at all, unless I was a tiny half-formed soul fluttering about in Heaven somewhere. When Edmund was about two years old Papa took the whole family to Switzerland and Germany, to spa towns where he hoped drinking the medicinal waters would help Mama to get better, though I can't see how drinking water could help somebody whose mind was diseased. They bought the children Swiss costumes and had their photographs taken, and that's all I have of the brother I never knew. One photograph of him in his tiny Swiss costume standing on a velvet chair. He has long curly hair and he looks rather cross, but people often do look cross in photographs, especially children, because it's hard to keep still for so long. In fact I think Edmund was a merry little fellow, and mischievous too; Papa told me that in the hotel

Edmund seized a bumper of wine and climbed onto the table with it, and held it aloft telling the other guests that 'the wine is good'! And all when he was only two years old!

Papa would sometimes mention Edmund; what a strong, brave boy he was, how he loved to ride on Papa's shoulders among the tall trees that grow round Scalands, Aunt Barbara's house, how delighted he was when Papa carried him that way backwards down the lanes. But I never heard him talk about Edmund's illness and death. Louisa, our parlourmaid, told me about it, just a little, but she made me promise not to tell Papa that she'd said anything. She told me that Edmund had diphtheria, which means that your throat gets very sore, and slowly it closes up so that you can't swallow, and eventually you can't even breathe. Sometimes the doctor bores a little hole into your throat to let air in, but they only do that if everything else has failed. Louisa said that when Edmund was ill, Papa hardly left his side. He fed him on tiny little pieces of pheasant and roasted apple, and then, when he couldn't swallow that, he tried to get him to swallow spoonfuls of meat jelly. But the day came when Edmund couldn't swallow anything at all, and couldn't speak, not even in a whisper, and then, said Louisa, 'Your Papa knew that all he could do was pray.'

Papa was with Edmund when he died. 'We all knew he'd gone straight to Heaven,' Louisa said, 'because he looked so beautiful and so peaceful.'

Edmund and Mama are buried in the same tomb. Papa's there now too, of course – somehow I keep forgetting that. The last time I visited it was on Harry's twenty-first birthday. Mabel was surprised that he wanted to pay such a sad visit on his birthday, but Harry said, 'It's right that I should be with my parents on the day I come of age.' So Mabel ordered the carriage – it still feels strange that Mabel is in charge of the household – and we set off for the graveyard. We left behind Harry's Oxford friends, who were staying at Yotes, but we took Willyboy with us because he's family.

Mabel laid a wreath of evergreens on the tomb, and we stood there in silence, absorbed in our own thoughts. Edmund, Mama, Papa. Are they quiet sleepers, I wonder? The tombstone is large; there is room for several more names.

There, that's quite enough of death and sorrow. This chapter's like a box; I've put all the sad things in it and fastened the lid. I'll make sure the next episode will be a little more exhilarating.

Never Say Die
March, 1883

And what could be more exhilarating than the story of Uncle Ben's Arctic adventure? I said at the beginning that I'd tell this tale, so now I will. This is the story of icebergs lit from within, glowing with unearthly colours, of waves rising up like cliff faces; of walruses and great white bears and a brave, clever dog called Bob; of the courage and endurance of Uncle Ben and his crew. It's also the story of all of us waiting at home almost stifled with anxiety – it was when Uncle Ben was missing that I understood the expression 'to have one's heart in one's mouth'. But there's no sorrow in the story, or almost none.

Uncle Ben is my hero, I suppose. My other hero is King

Charles I, but he belongs in history and . . . well, I won't go on about my feelings for King Charles now, because they can get rather too romantic! But King Charles is dead and Uncle Ben is alive and well, thank goodness.

Uncle Ben isn't only *my* hero. When he came back from the Arctic, his picture was in all the papers, and he was congratulated by the Queen, and given a gold medal. I thought I would burst with pride, but Uncle Ben didn't want any of it. He said he dreaded fame 'more than ice'. The Royal Geographical Society asked him to give a talk to a big audience of important people, to tell them all about his travels, and Uncle Ben said he would, but at the last minute he found he couldn't do it, and someone else had to give his talk for him.

My uncle has no wife or children. Mabel, who's very bold, asked him why not, and he replied that he was married to the sea. Well, all I can say is that at times she's been a very difficult wife. Uncle Ben has led five expeditions to the Arctic regions. I always used to hope that he would find the North Pole, and bring back the old man who sits there holding his lantern, for that is what I used to believe. He never did reach the North Pole – so perhaps that old man is sitting there still, though my nearly fifteen-year-old self rather doubts it! –

but he explored all sorts of islands and stretches of coastline that nobody had ever seen before, and he brought back things for scientists in London to study – fossils, seabirds' eggs, rare plants, even white bears for the Zoological Gardens in Regent's Park! Once, on board ship, one of the bears escaped from his cage on the deck and nearly dived back into the sea, but Uncle Ben fell on him and wrestled him back into his cage. They named this bear Sampson, after one of Uncle Ben's ships. Sampson still lives at the zoo. I went to visit him not so long ago. I held out a currant bun speared on the tip of Creathy's umbrella, and he stood up and lifted it off and ate it in the most obliging manner.

Another time, Uncle Ben and his crew went to the rescue of a Swedish expedition. The Swedish ship was stuck fast in the ice, I believe, and had run out of supplies. Uncle Ben's ship broke through, somehow, and brought food and medicine to those poor stranded men and took them home. Poor fellows, they must have wondered if they would ever see their homes again. Is it not a grand thing, to have saved all those lives?

I remember hearing the news of that rescue. I was five years old; it was a few months after Mama's death. The cousins were all gathered together here at Yotes Court, and the grown-ups were endlessly discussing Uncle Ben's return; nobody knew where he was or when to expect him. Mabel had written a play; it was called *Never Say Die*, and we children were acting it out for the grown-ups. I was the littlest one then, except for Lionel, who must have been a baby; Bella and Dolly had not even been born. I was so proud to be taking my part in the play alongside Roddy and Willyboy, who seemed to me so terribly clever. On the very evening that we were to act it, we heard wheels scrunching on the gravel sweep in front of the house. 'Who can be calling at this late hour?' demanded Papa, a little vexed. He did not like irregularity. Then the double doors to the drawing room flew open and in came Uncle Ben! His ship had docked that very morning, and he had travelled all day to see us children before we were sent to bed.

His face was dark, the colour, almost, of our mahogany dining table. Cold and wind can change the colour of your skin, as well as sun. Against that dark skin his eyes looked impossibly blue. He had very little luggage of his own – Uncle Willy had to lend him a clean suit of clothes – but he had bundles of presents for everyone. For Mabel and me he had wolverine skins, dark underneath and silvery on top;

I had never felt anything so soft and warm. Creathy made them up into tippets and muffs for us. To Harry he gave a narwhal's tusk, a noble length of ivory, just as I imagined a unicorn's horn would look.

Uncle Ben didn't know about our play. Once he had done hugging us and throwing us in the air if we were small enough – which I certainly was – he turned to talk and drink sherry wine with the adults, and we put our heads together in a corner and whispered. We added a scene to the play where Willyboy came in as a messenger and read out a pretend report in *The Times* telling of 'the successful Polar expedition of Mr Benjamin Leigh Smith'. When we acted our play all the audience clapped especially hard, and Uncle Ben's roars of laughter could have been heard, I'm sure, all over Mereworth.

Uncle Ben could name the places he discovered just as he chose, so he named them after his relations. There's Cape Leigh Smith and Cape Ludlow, for everyone in the family. There's Bell Island, which happens to be shaped like a bell, but 'Bell' is what Uncle Ben always called my mama. Mabel has a whole island to herself – Mabel Island. As for me – well, I've just got a little place named after me, a bay on Mabel Island called Milicent Bay. I don't mind that I'm just a little part of Mabel's place. That's rather how it feels in real life – that I'm quite a little thing, engulfed, sometimes, by my grown-up sister. Mabel still tucks me up at night. If she's going out to a ball or a dinner, she sits on my bed and I embrace her very carefully so as not to disturb her jewels or her hair, and I enjoy the smell of her perfume mixed with the scent of the gardenia that she wears pinned in her bosom. Papa didn't like her to wear perfume, but Uncle Ben bought it for her when he took her to Paris, so she had to be allowed to use it.

I like that cosy feeling of being tucked up in bed, and when I'm drifting off to sleep I like to imagine my Arctic bay. Uncle Ben has described it to me; the icebergs like floating castles, the sky full of strange colours; green, purple and violet, the grey rocks softened by splats of yellow lichen like broken eggs; the one tiny brave flower, pinkish in colour, that clings to the cliffs in what they call their summer, which is still colder than most of our winter days; the seabirds – thousands upon thousands – which scream and squabble all over the cliff faces; the cliffs rising steep like frowning foreheads then levelling off like a broad table top. It is a lonely, inhospitable place, but Uncle Ben says it has a beauty of its own, and when I imagine the cries of the wind and the waves and the seabirds I feel snugger than ever under my heavy blankets.

Some people in our family begged Ben to stop risking his life on these voyages, to settle down and make a home and take a wife like a sensible fellow. But my uncle could not rest while there were still new worlds to conquer. He built himself a ship, designed in exactly the best way to withstand ice, and he named her Eira, which means 'snow' in Welsh, I believe. Two years ago, in 1881, he set off in the *Eira* with his sturdy crew of Scotch sailors, Bob the woolly coated retriever, a tabby cat, and a canary in a cage.

They set sail in June; they were expected back by the end of September. Papa became more and more concerned as the autumn sped by without a sign of them. He tried not to worry us, but when he asked me whether I always remembered Uncle Ben in my nightly prayers, I understood how serious things were.

Mabel's birthday falls on the first of December. Papa took her into Tunbridge Wells to choose a gold watch, but she said that the best present she could possibly have would be news of Uncle Ben. We celebrated her birthday – her twenty-first – with a grand dinner party and a bonfire and fireworks in the garden, but still there was no word of the *Eira*.

People began to say that a search party should be sent. Such an expedition couldn't set out until the spring, because there was too much ice – no ship would be able to get through. Papa and Uncle Willy wrote letters to the government, explaining what was needed and why, but the government wouldn't supply enough money, which made me wish, like Aunt Barbara, that women were allowed to vote, so that when I was old enough I could vote against the government if it was still in power. I said this to Aunt Bar and she made a face that was half a smile and half sad, and she said, 'Oh my dear, when women get the vote, I will be in my winding sheet and you will be a grandmother leaning on a stick!'

A fund was set up to raise money for the search party. Uncle Ben's friends and relations all gave what they could. Harry was put in charge of collecting the money and adding it up. He told me that Papa, Aunt Nanny and Aunt Barbara each put in a thousand pounds.

At last enough money was raised, and a friend of Uncle Ben's called Sir Allen Young set sail in search of the *Eira*. We wrote letters for Sir Allen to give to Uncle Ben, if he should find him, and I gave each letter a kiss for luck and as I did so I imagined that I was pressing my lips upon my uncle's brown cheek. Mabel went to see the rescue ship set sail, but I wasn't allowed to go because, forsooth, it would disrupt my schoolwork too much! This brought forth a most unladylike fit of temper on my part, I'm afraid! Sir Allen's ship was called the *Hope*, which felt like a good name.

I tried to put it all out of my mind, for I knew it would be weeks, if not months, before we heard any news. But all through that summer – last summer – I kept having dreams about Uncle Ben. Once I dreamed that he and I were dancing together on a flat sheet of ice, and I was wearing my thin dancing slippers, and the ice split in half with a most horrid creaking groan, and Uncle Ben was carried further and further away until he was a tiny figure on the horizon, but still he kept on dancing. Then I woke up with a jolt, and found that somehow my feet were sticking out from under the bedclothes, and they were icy cold!

We had no news until late in August. Then out of the blue, as they say, a telegram arrived: 'Crew all safe but *Eira* is awa. Ben.' Awa is the word the Scotch sailors would have used. What had happened was that the *Eira* had sunk!

Slowly, we got to know the whole story. Miss Isabella Blythe, who is Aunt Nanny's very dear friend – we call her Isa – wrote down Ben's adventures in a long letter, which was sent round to everyone in the family. Let me see how much I can remember . . .

The expedition had been going well, and they'd collected all sorts of interesting specimens to bring back to London. But the ice wasn't behaving itself. It set in much earlier than they had ever known it, and the *Eira* got stuck fast between a mass of ice and the land. The men did not realise how fast the ice was moving. They were on shore, looking about them, when one of them cried, 'She's sinking!' A great hole had opened in the *Eira*'s side, and water was pouring in. The men broke the glass in the portholes and worked as hard as they could to save things before she went down. They had two hours, or not even that. They saved food in tins, rum, beer and Champagne, guns and ammunition, the rowing boats, and of course Bob, the cat, and the canary. They cut up the *Eira*'s masts to use the wood. They also saved some big white damask tablecloths, like the ones we use on the long dining table here at Yotes. What need would you have for damask tablecloths when you are shipwrecked in the Arctic?

You may well ask. But those tablecloths came in very handy, as you shall hear.

What else did they save? Curry powder, a few currants, Uncle Ben's musical box . . . an odd jumble of things, but all the precious fossils and plants and notebooks and maps were lost.

At last the men had to jump from the deck to the shore to save their lives. Within minutes, the *Eira* was below the surface of the water. They saw her clearly just for a moment, lying on the seabed, and then the ice closed over and she was lost to view. 'Poor old Eira,' said Uncle Ben, and after that he did not speak of her again.

The captain of the ship (for Uncle Ben was the leader of the expedition, not the captain of the ship) started giving orders to the men, but they muttered amongst themselves. 'The ship has gone; you're not our captain any more. We can do as we please,' they said. Ben stepped forward. 'I can do without you better than you can do without me,' he told them. 'If you will do as I say, and obey me and, through me, Captain Lofley, then I will lead you all to safety. If you do not, you will perish. The choice is yours.' The sailors were so impressed by the firmness of his tone and the strength of his look, and by the way that he'd worked harder than any of them to save things from the sinking ship, that they agreed to follow his orders, and they gave him three hearty cheers.

They found a patch of green, in a crevice between some rocks, and under Uncle Ben's instructions they set about making a hut with mud, stones and the wood they had salvaged from the wreck. Uncle Ben named the hut Flora Cottage, after our cousin Flora. They built a smaller hut to store the meat in, from the animals they hunted. Uncle Ben ordered that all the tinned food should be saved, for he knew that when the ice broke up the following spring they would have to get into the longboats and attempt to row for home, and they would need the tinned food to survive that journey. So all through the long, long winter when they were living in Flora Cottage they were obliged to shoot seabirds and walruses and polar bears for their food.

Uncle Ben was the best shot. If my papa had been with him, he might have been even better; Papa and Uncle Ben and Uncle Willy often used to go out shooting pheasants and partridges together, and all agreed that Papa was the best shot, in spite of the old-fashioned muzzle-loader that he used. But Uncle Ben was good too, and in the Arctic it was usually he who went out after the great white bears, with the faithful Bob by his side. All the men owe their lives to Bob. Many times a man would fall into icy water when out hunting walruses or scavenging for something to burn in the stove they made, and Bob would run back to the hut to fetch help if he could not pull the man out of the water himself. When Uncle Ben was hunting bears, Bob would run on ahead, barking, and draw a bear nearer to him, until it was within range of Uncle Ben's gun, and then Bob would slip away to safety while the shot was fired.

I do not like to think of those noble bears being tricked and shot, but if the men were to survive they had no choice. If the bears were left with nothing but men to eat, I'm sure they would return the compliment! When the men cut up the bears, they were careful to save the blood. A pint of bear's blood wonderfully enriched a soup or a stew, we learned, though it's a recipe I hope I never have to follow myself. If the bear had recently been feeding on a seal, its stomach would be full of oil and this, apparently, made excellent cooking oil!

And so they spent the long, dark winter months; in December and January there is not really any daylight at all. The bears' skins were important in preventing them from freezing to death. They listened to the musical box until it froze, and on Christmas Day they drank Champagne and ate a tiny Christmas pudding made from the flour and currants they had managed to save. But they all kept as cheerful as they could, and held services every Sunday, and mostly they were healthy. There was one poor fellow who had a cancer on his lip, and often he was in terrible pain, but he took his turn at the chores with all the rest. Another man lost part of his arm in an accident. But they all survived that long, long winter.

In March, Uncle Ben became very worried, though he hid his fears as best he could. The seabirds were getting scarcer and scarcer, frightened off, perhaps, by the guns, which at first had taken them by surprise. The bears, too, were getting harder to find, as they moved away in search of prey or hid in their underground lairs with their young. One day Uncle Ben realised that the only food they had left were the precious tinned supplies that were essential for their return journey. Uncle Ben is not a church-goer – Papa always used to say what a pity that was – but he is a religious man in his way, because he lay down in his berth at Flora Cottage and turned his face to the wall and said the Lord's Prayer. Then he got up and went out and shot a bear almost straight away.

On Queen Victoria's birthday – May 23rd – they

celebrated with singing, dancing and Champagne! It was not long after this that the ice began to break up, and Uncle Ben knew they must take their chance on the wild and treacherous seas. There were six men to each boat, but seven in Uncle Ben's, for he took the poor cancer man with him. They left behind the musical box and some bottles of Champagne. They took dear Bob with them, of course, but they drowned the cat. That seems sad to me, but perhaps the sailors thought she would bring bad luck, or perhaps she would not have sat still in the rowing boats. The poor little canary had long since perished of the cold.

They lived on the tinned food they had saved from the wreck of the *Eira*. They rowed for so many miles – I think it was eight hundred – and sometimes the waves were thirty feet high and threatened to engulf them, but they were strong, stout-hearted fellows and they pulled through. Even the poor fellow with only one arm took his turn at an oar. And this is when the tablecloths came in handy – remember I told you they saved the tablecloths? Well, they hoist them as sails, and got along far more quickly than they could have done by rowing alone.

After 'contending with the fretful elements' for ever so long, at least five weeks I think, they came within hail of the rescue ship the *Hope*, and you can imagine what a mighty cheer went up! They were all got safely aboard; Sir Allen Young said their faces were nearly black, and they had a powerful smell of fish about them! The *Hope* took them back to Aberdeen, where the cancer man was put straight into hospital (but he died a few days later, poor soul) and the men were all united with their wives and children, who must have given up hope of ever seeing them again.

And it wasn't long before Uncle Ben came to see us. His face was the colour of beaten copper, and there were grey streaks in his beard, but otherwise he was the same Uncle Ben I remember from my earliest days. Papa shook him by the hand long and hard; he could hardly speak. 'My dear Ben,' he kept repeating. 'So glad – so glad.'

When Papa died, only three months later, one of the consoling things Aunt Bar said to me was how fortunate it was that he'd lived long enough to see Ben's safe return. That is true. And Papa must have known, too, that if anything happened to him, Uncle Ben would take care of us. Harry says Uncle Ben is *in loco parentis*, which means 'in place of a parent'. Mabel thinks that she's too old to need a guardian, but I'm glad that Uncle Ben's in charge of us. As I told you before, he is my hero.

Hare and Hounds
March, 1883

My birthday is fast approaching. Fifteen! How ancient!

The day itself is 8th March. We will have a dinner party to celebrate, with dancing afterwards. Miss Kahn will play the dance tunes on the piano for us. I expect I will have regained my energy by then, but right now I don't feel as if I could dance a single step!

I'm writing this in my dressing-gown, while my bath is drawn. Usually I take my tub in the morning, but I came in in such a state from our excessively dramatic game of 'Hare and Hounds' that Creathy ordered a bath immediately and she's going to wash my hair, too, to get the duckweed out of it. I hate hair-washing. I feel giddy, turning my head upside down to dry it in front of my bedroom fire, and it takes so long.

'Hare and Hounds' . . . oh, I really should begin at the beginning, shouldn't I? Mabel and Harry are making quite a 'thing' of my birthday. Harry has taken leave of absence from Oxford to be here. I wonder if he'll get into trouble? If so, I expect he'll manage to charm his way out of it. Everyone likes Harry. I don't see why the 'powers that be' at Oxford should be any exception. It's something to do with his curly hair, and his dimples. When I was little he used to tell me that he'd been shot through both cheeks with an arrow, and that the dimples were the scars, and do you know what? I believed him!

The excitement began yesterday, at tea-time. I was struggling with a French composition when I heard a commotion in the hall, doors slamming and boots flung down, instructions shouted to the stable boy, and squeals of laughter from Mabel in her most high-pitched mode. I threw down my pen, ruining my work with a spatter of ink, and ran downstairs to find Harry and his friend Mr Arthur Glover, arrived a day earlier than expected, to surprise us.

'Little sister!' cried Harry, stretching wide his arms. As he swept me off my feet, I caught sight of Mabel helping Mr Glover off with his coat. Her cheeks were pink and her eyes were bright. It is really the job of Louisa, our parlourmaid, to take the coats. I looked in surprise at Louisa, who was standing at a respectful distance, and was even more surprised when she gave me a wink.

'Louisa, serve tea here, in front of the fire, if you please,' instructed Mabel. The young men were ravenous after their journey – they'd ridden all the way from London. Louisa brought pikelets dripping with melted butter, but Mabel had to ring twice for fresh batches. Mr Glover stretched himself out, his hands behind his head. He's taller than Harry, and broader, and he seemed to take up a lot of space, even in our big hall. He has crinkly yellow hair, a ruddy face, and strong-looking white teeth; I expect most people would consider him a fine-looking fellow, but I'm not sure that I do. There were gouts of melted butter glistening on his broad, square chin.

'Well, Miss Ludlow,' he said to Mabel. 'You certainly know how to look after a chap. Pikelets – my word! And is that a seedcake I spy?'

'Let me order something more substantial, Mr Glover. Louisa! Soft-boiled eggs and toast for the gentlemen, if you please.'

'Not forgetting the ladies,' put in Harry. 'Little Mil, you'd like an egg, would you not?'

I shook my head, and blushed. I had given up afternoon tea for Lent – at least, I allowed myself to drink a cup, but I would not eat a morsel save for plain, dry bread. Mabel laughed, with an edge of scorn. 'Oh, Harry, you know what a pious little thing she is. She's given up eggs for Lent, along with goodness knows how many other things. She quite disapproves of my indulgent ways, and thinks we should all be "mortifying the flesh"!'

I did not like the way Mabel talked about me as though I was not there, and I disliked even more her using the word 'flesh' in the presence of Mr Glover. It seemed almost indecent. I gazed resolutely into the fire, and said nothing.

'Milicent always did put the two of us to shame, Mabel,' said Harry. 'But can we forget Lent for tomorrow, do you suppose? Girls, what do you say to a game of Hare and Hounds?'

'Oh, do let's!' I exclaimed, forgetting my annoyance. We had not played at Hare and Hounds since long before Papa's death, and I do love it so. It's a chasing game, in case you've forgotten. All you need to play is a large space, some scraps of paper, and a group of energetic people.

The park at Yotes is perfect. The youngest players are the hares; they set off in advance, leaving a trail of torn-up paper. When you've run out of paper, or out of breath, you hide. The 'hounds' – that is, everyone who is not a hare – set off in search of you. They sound a hunting horn; you hear them getting closer – or further off – and the noise is rather thrilling.

'Milicent, fetch my writing things,' demanded my sister, and for once I didn't object to being ordered about because I knew she intended to dispatch notes to our neighbours, inviting them to take part.

And so this afternoon, after an early luncheon, nine hounds assembled in the turning circle in front of the house, chattering and laughing, giving the hares – Evelyn Stapleton and me – a chance to get away. Evelyn and I each had a leather satchel over our shoulders, crammed with scraps of paper. We set off at a trot up the avenue, scattering as we went.

When we turned into the road that leads to Mereworth, we became devious. I am quicker than Evelyn, so I laid a trail to make it look as if we had turned the corner into the village, while she did the same to the stile into the far field. Then we both doubled back and scrambled over the park wall. Just then we heard the first call of the horn. To cross the open parkland would be a risk. We ducked down by the wall, and clutched each other, stifling our giggles, as we listened to the hounds tramping off in the wrong direction.

'Where next?' we asked each other when it seemed safe to venture out. 'Let's go to the lake,' suggested Evelyn, 'we want them to think we've drowned. In fact, I would rather like to half-drown, because then I could be rescued.' At the water's edge we paused, panting a little. Branches of hazel trailed over it, the dangling catkins tickling the surface; the rusty orange of the sallow twigs contrasted pleasingly with the pale-blue March sky. 'What a pretty subject for a sketch!' I said.

Evelyn poked a stick into the water. 'You and your sketches. Ooh, look, Mil, frogspawn! I wish we'd brought a jar.'

'We wouldn't be very effective hares, carrying frogspawn,' said I. We both gazed at the little island in the middle of the lake, the ruins of the monastery walls humped like lumps of old bread. 'The perfect hiding place!' Evelyn declared. She was serious. A small flat-bottomed boat was kept moored to the landing stage, and there were two paddles in it.

'We'd never be found,' I objected. 'How could the hounds get across, if we took the boat?

'Hounds can swim.'

'Well, hares can't row.'

'These hares can. Come on, Mil. You always say we don't have enough adventures.' Evelyn was already tugging at the painter to launch the boat. I could see I had no choice. We climbed in, and after a couple of wobbles and splashes we were off. Evelyn insisted on leaving a trail of paper scraps behind us on the water, even though the ripples dispersed them at once. I was worried that ducks would swallow them and choke, but Evelyn said, 'Oh no, they'll use them to line their nests.'

We managed the little journey well, and scrambled ashore with no harm done save for a few snags to our pinafores where the brambles snatched at them. I tied the painter to a stout branch, as Harry had taught me, then we set up camp in the ruins of the monastery. We trampled down last year's fox-coloured bracken for a couch, and used our satchels as pillows. Then we lay down and waited. Evelyn pulled a bag of peppermint humbugs from the pocket of her pinafore. 'Let's pretend it's not Lent,' she said, and I agreed.

'Who do you hope catches us?' Evelyn asked, as we sucked.

I cast my mind over the chattering group that had assembled in front of the house. Roger and Sylvia Dalison, the Stackpole girls, Evelyn's older brother Hugh and sister Nellie, Harry, Mabel, and of course Mr Glover. I knew Evelyn wanted me to choose Hugh, who is nineteen and will probably become a clergyman like his father. When Evelyn and I discuss our futures, Evelyn says to me, 'If all else fails, you can always marry Hugh,' and I know she means well, but I wish his chin stuck out a little more and his teeth a little less. I said, 'I don't know. Harry, I suppose. Not Mr Dalison – I'll leave him for Nellie,' and we both laughed, because it was generally believed that Roger Dalison was 'sweet' on Nellie Stapleton, but she would have nothing to do with him.

'I hope it's Mr Glover,' announced Evelyn. 'If he finds me, he can keep me, if he likes.'

'Evelyn Stapleton!' I was shocked. 'What a forward girl you are!'

'Mr Glover is a very good-looking man, Milicent. He has such splendid teeth. Surely you agree?'

Just then we heard the call of the hunting horn, and

the voices of the hounds, so I was spared an answer. We both hissed 'Sssh!' to each other, and snuggled down in the bracken. The conversation of our pursuers drifted clearly across the lake. 'They can't be on the island!' That was Nellie's voice. Then Harry – 'They are! Look, the boat's gone. The little rapscallions!'

'If the boat's gone, we can't reach them,' said Mabel, a little too decisively. 'Let us return to the house. They will soon discover that their plan was a foolish one.'

'Oh, but Mabel,' put in tender-hearted Sylvia Dalison. 'We can't leave them. They might drown.'

'Have they drowned already?' said Hugh Stapleton. 'There is a great deal of paper on the surface of the water.' At that, Evelyn gently pinched my arm in triumph.

'Hares! Where are you hiding?' Arthur Glover's deep voice rang out across the water.

'We must show ourselves,' I whispered. 'How else can they find us?' Evelyn shook her head. 'Let's creep back to the boat, and take them by surprise.'

The boat's mooring place was sheltered by scrubby bushes, elder and hawthorn, so the suggestion was not absurd. On our hands and knees, our satchels hanging about our necks, we crawled out of the ruins. Despite prickles and mud, we reached the boat without attracting attention, slipped the knot, and drifted off. But at the first movement of our paddles a shout went up from the bank. 'There they are! Grab them the moment they're ashore!' And then Evelyn, for some unaccountable reason, took it upon herself to attempt to turn the boat without warning me. Our paddles, having been in harmony, were at war with each other; there was a tremendous wobble, and the next thing I knew, water was over my head, filling my eyes, ears and mouth.

It felt like an eternity, but it can't have been more than a few seconds before strong hands grasped me and hauled me above the surface. It wasn't until we reached the bank that I realised my rescuer was Mr Glover. I could hardly thank him, my teeth were chattering so hard.

'I'll carry her home,' said Harry, but Mr Glover intervened. 'I'm wet through already,' he pointed out. 'No need for anyone else to get soaked.' And he scooped me up and set off at a surprising rate. I was obliged to fasten my arms round his neck; the warmth of his breath on my cheek was disconcerting. As we jolted away I caught sight of Evelyn – who, by some miracle, had *not* fallen in – and the look on her face was so transparently jealous, it nearly made me laugh aloud.

I was less deeply in disgrace with Creathy than I thought I would be, mostly because Evelyn, who's a brick, took all the blame on herself. The extent of my punishment was that, even after I was warm and dry, I was not allowed to join the others downstairs. I knew they were all in the hall being fed on bread and cheese and brawn and plumcake, and drinking hot stirrup cup, before they dispersed, but I was quite happy to keep away from them, because I dreaded the spats of chafing and rib-digging that would doubtless have erupted on my appearance. Besides, I wanted to sit quietly and think in peace. Amidst all the excitement I had not forgotten the date. 6th March. Ten years since my mama was taken from us.

Creathy had ordered me to remain in my room, but I knew that she would be occupied for some time, sorting out my wet things. I had gathered a little nosegay of celandines and wood anemones that morning in the orchard and set them in my painting jar. I took the jar, slipped downstairs and, easing the heavy door open as quietly as I could, I entered Papa's study, where the marble bust of Mama stands.

I almost dropped the flowers when I realised I was not alone. The room was shuttered, but in the twilight I could make out a figure kneeling in front of the bust, head bowed as if in prayer. I thought of the legend of the ghost I had never seen, and for a moment my limbs turned to ice, but then I saw the outline of Harry's curly head. I said not a word, but knelt down quietly by his side.

He took the posy from my hand, and placed it next to our cold white marble mother. 'I didn't think of flowers,' he said. 'Well done, little sister.' He stretched out an arm and drew me to him. Sometimes I think my brother understands me better than anybody else.

The Diamond Band
March, 1883

And now the great day has dawned, as they say in books. In fact it has more than dawned. I have *not* caught pneumonia, despite Creathy's dire predictions; no, I am full of beans, and I am in my bedroom, where I have been sent to 'rest' before my birthday dinner. Mabel won't tell me what is on the menu, but she knows I am very fond of lobster, so I think that will appear, if there is any to be had. Mabel, I know, will take pleasure in breaking my Lenten resolutions. But in any case I had made up my mind to do so. I can't believe that Our Lord would want me to spoil my birthday dinner, for His sake.

At five o'clock Creathy will help me dress and do my

hair – I am to put it 'up' for the first time – and then my 'rest' will end. Not that rest is possible on such an exciting day, so I am occupying my time in writing this. And because it's my birthday, it seems a good day to write about myself. I've told you, my future self – or should I say, *reminded* you? – about my house and garden and quite a lot about my family, but I think I will jog your memory, now, about the harum-scarum girl you once were.

I know I'm not a pretty girl. Perhaps that's why Evelyn and I are such great friends, because she's not pretty either. She wouldn't mind my saying that; she says so herself. Her face is round and doughy, and her eyes are small, like currants pressed into the dough, though she has a merry smile and a neat little nose. Evelyn is rather plump all over, but I'm small, and thin. I don't think I've stopped growing yet, but I don't suppose I'll ever be as tall as my sister. People call Mabel 'a fine girl'. She holds herself very straight, she moves gracefully, like the expert dancer she is, and she loves new clothes. Uncle Ben had a ballgown made for her last birthday. She hasn't been able to wear it until today, because we are still wearing black for Papa, but tonight we are going to come out of mourning, just for my birthday.

Mabel's gown is of ivory satin, with pink silk rosebuds at the neck and shoulders. It falls to the ground in ripples, like a waterfall arrested in mid flow. Mabel has beautiful arms, rounded and creamy-white. My arms are thin, like a scarecrow's. Mabel's hair is thicker than mine, and fairer too. Cousin Amy told her that if she anointed it with lemon juice it would become fairer still; that was when Papa was alive, and wasn't he cross when she picked lemons from the trees in the glasshouse without permission. But, being Papa, he wasn't cross for long.

Sometimes she plaits it and winds it round her head like a crown, as Aunt Barbara has taught her. Aunt Barbara's hair is famous. When she was young it was a mass of rippling red-gold. It was admired by the artist Dante Gabriel Rossetti. He loved to paint hair like that. But I'm moving away from the subject. I said I was going to tell you about myself, and I keep talking about other people in the family! But that's right in a way because those people are part of me. I can't think of myself as separate from my family. I suppose you could call us a clan.

I have inherited some of the family characteristics. I am determined (some would say stubborn) and I like painting and flowers and books and music, as do my aunts and cousins. But I have not inherited the family hair! Amy with her glossy chestnut braids, piled up high; little Bella with her shiny curls, even baby Dolly already has a cloud of fair fluff. Why, oh why, is my hair thin, wispy and the exact colour of the dullest kind of dead leaf – a pale nothingy brown? Not content with being dull, my hair is also disobedient. When I tie it up, little bits escape and blow all over the place. I must confess that I am not by nature a tidy girl. My bootlaces untie themselves, my shawl is for ever slipping off my shoulders and I am always losing buttons, so I suppose I shouldn't blame my hair for following suit.

Mabel's eyes are large and china-blue and set rather far apart. My eyes are grey. Papa used to say they were the colour of the English Channel. He said he liked that colour because he felt so happy when he reached the Channel on the last stage of his journey home from India. My eyes aren't small, but they're deep-set and close together, and unkind people, including my dear brother Harry, say I look as if I'm squinting.

Mabel's nose is short and straight, and her chin is round, with a dimple in it. My nose seems to go on for ever, with a funny bump in it, and my chin is narrow and pointed.

Aunt Bar calls me her little elf-child, which is her kind way of making my lack of prettiness into something interesting. But Aunt Jenny, who thought I was such a beautiful baby, has altered her opinion over the last fifteen years. I overheard her describe me to Aunt Bar as 'such a dried-up little thing'.

I haven't been very kind to myself, have I? Perhaps I should find something to praise. Well, 'here goes', to use a vulgar expression. I have elegant eyebrows, like delicate pencil marks. Did any man ever fall in love with a pair of eyebrows, I wonder? Could he gaze on them, and overlook the bumpy nose and the squint?

I like my hands, too. The fingernails are almond-shaped, and my fingers are slender and dainty. They are not lily-white, however, which is how a lady's hands should be. I look quite peculiar when I'm in my tub because my hands are brown and the rest of me is white. Of course I'm supposed to wear gloves at all times, but I can't bear gloves when the sun's shining and I'm running about in the long grass picking flowers, so I take them off and stuff them in my pocket, and Creathy says, 'Miss Milicent! I declare, you're turning into a gypsy girl!'

When I'm sure that Creathy's a very long way off,

I remove my boots and stockings too and run about with bare feet. I remember a glorious day when I was very little and Aunt Bar came to stay and brought the beautiful Amy with her, and Aunt Bar persuaded us all to paddle barefoot in the watercress beds that lie between our park and the surrounding farmland. The dark water was so cool and delicious! Amy's hair shook itself free as she splashed and laughed; it tumbled about her shoulders and she looked like a wood nymph with her bare feet and her big, dark eyes.

Sometimes I wish I were a gypsy girl. When the gypsies come to Yotes to pick hops in September I love to steal little glimpses into their caravans. Everything is painted in such gay colours, and is so cunningly fitted and stowed away. How I would love to travel up and down the country in a caravan pulled by a jolly skewbald horse, and cook in the open air, and settle down to sleep wherever I fetched up, on fine nights lying under the stars! Yotes Court is the only home I've ever known, and I love it, and I know my life there is comfortable and safe, but there's a part of me that yearns for danger and adventure.

Not many people know I have that yearning. The birthday presents I received today show that most people regard me as a respectable young lady! Mabel had arranged the parcels so prettily on the breakfast table, to greet me when I came downstairs. They were all fanned out round a jar of Lent lilies, the tiny pale daffodils that come before their robust yellow sisters. 'Fair daffodils, that come before the swallow dares, and take the winds of March with beauty' – that's from *The Winter's Tale*. Aunt Barbara has always made sure I know my Shakespeare.

Mabel's present to me was a jet necklace, which was thoughtful because I can wear it while we are still in mourning for Papa. Miss Kahn gave me a notebook, prettily bound, its leather cover embossed with a pattern of wild roses. Miss Kahn knows I like to write things down. Harry gave me *Chaplet of Pearls*, a novel by Mrs Yonge, my favourite author. With it he enclosed a comic sketch he'd made of himself wobbling down the High at Oxford on his penny-farthing bicycle.

My dear friend Evelyn gave me a prayer book. I knew that I should quell the faint sense of disappointment I felt when I opened this parcel, and I did so, and was rewarded when out of the prayer book fluttered a most beautiful picture, a garden scene cunningly made out of pressed flowers, and I recognised the flowers as those we had gathered together last summer. Evelyn's little brother

Frank gave me a pincushion with my initials made rather shakily in pins.

There were several other things. A book called *Lives of the Poets* from Aunt Bar, a gold sovereign from Uncle Ben, a length of Arab embroidery from Aunt Nanny, a silver brooch shaped like a crescent moon from Aunt Nanny's friend Isa, a box of butterscotch and a lace handkerchief from Creathy. A letter from Aunt Jenny explaining that she couldn't possibly find me a present as Lionel had chicken pox and Cook had just given in her notice. I could tell that everybody wanted two things for me on my birthday; first, to make me feel like a young lady, not a child, and second, to distract my attention from the fact that this was my first birthday without Papa.

Now it's nearly five o'clock and I hear Creathy's heavy footfall on the stairs. She's coming to help me dress. My white muslin gown with the lavender ribbons is hanging on the back of the door; the curling tongs are waiting on the dressing table like a medieval instrument of torture. So I must put down my pen, attempt to rub the ink off my fingers with a pumice stone and transform my gypsy self into an elegant young lady fit to receive her honoured birthday guests.

It's two o'clock in the morning! I'm writing as quickly as I can – Creathy thinks I've put my candle out. I don't think I've ever stayed up so late before. This has been a birthday to remember, in all sorts of ways.

I'm not usually shy, but when Creathy had finished with me, and my hair was all scraped upwards tugging at the skin on my face and leaving my poor thin neck exposed like a – well, not like a swan, unless perhaps one that has been plucked, and my skirts were billowing out round me, lifted by layers of scratchy, starchy petticoats, then, yes, I did feel shy. Creathy said, 'There! You look like a princess!' as she pinned a spray of lilies of the valley to my shoulder. But I didn't feel like a princess. I felt like some helpless little creature trapped inside a hot-air balloon, if you can imagine such a thing. At that moment I would gladly have flung open the window and floated up into the night sky in my ballooning skirts, rather than go downstairs and greet my guests.

Wrapping the wolverine skin that Uncle Ben gave me round my shivering shoulders, I leaned out of the window as far as I dared. Burning braziers had been set the whole length of the avenue, to guide the carriages. The orange dots of flame stretched out like the beads of a necklace. To my horror I saw a vehicle proceeding up the drive – so soon, far too early! But when it reached the turning circle in front of the house I was relieved to recognise the Rectory brougham, bringing the Stapletons. Our dearest friends hardly count as guests! Forgetting my shyness, and casting the wolverine aside, I hurried down to greet them.

'Miss Milicent! Not so quick! You'll untidy yourself!' called Creathy, and indeed I had to slow my pace out of deference to my rustling skirts and the heavy piled-up hair that felt precarious despite the insertion of what seemed like a thousand hair pins. I descended the wide staircase in stately fashion, one hand on the banister, the other gathering my skirts. And then I had the strangest experience. Somehow, I caught sight of my reflection in the long gilt-framed mirror that hangs in the hall, and there I was super-imposed on the reflection of the portrait of that lady in green, the lady with the pearls and the damaged face. Perhaps it was a trick of the light – the leaping shadows thrown up by the hall fire that I had never seen heaped so high before. But there was my face, just exactly filling the shape of that long-ago ruined face, and for that instant, I was her. I couldn't help but let out a little scream.

Just in time I converted the scream into a whoop of joy with which to greet the young Stapletons; Nellie, Hugh, and of course Evelyn. Little Frank, to his fury I was told, was deemed too young for such a party.

'My goodness!' exclaimed Nellie, who, as the nearest in age to Mabel, is considered her special friend, despite their frequent squabbles. 'Mabel *has* gone to town! Whatever would your dear papa have thought?' She waved her hand at the candles. Every sconce and chandelier in the hall and the two drawing rooms, now opened out into one, glittered with its full complement of tall white candles. The draught from the newly opened front doors had set their crystal droplets twirling and spinning; they cast jewelled shadows on the walls, moving splashes of amethyst, sapphire and topaz. I thought of that story about the twelve dancing princesses and their palace underground; indeed, the flickering shadows made it seem as if the house was full of phantom dancers.

I knew what Nellie meant when she asked what our papa would have thought. My father gave generously to charity, but in his domestic habits he was so frugal that the standing joke among the Stapletons was that he would allow Yotes to be lit only by a single candle. And tonight Mabel certainly had 'gone to town'. The resinous scent of the burning logs mingled with the rich yet delicate hothouse flowers – lilac and hyacinths, jonquils and gardenias – that spilled out of the immense stone urns, intertwined with trailing fronds of ivy. There is nothing more beautiful in nature than a glossy new ivy leaf.

'All this for you, little Lilybel!' said Hugh, bowing low and kissing my white-gloved hand. I tried not to flinch.

'Well,' murmured Nellie as if to herself. 'Is it *quite* all for Milicent?' I don't think she intended me to hear, but I did. I followed her gaze to the staircase, down which descended Arthur Glover and Harry, resplendent in white tie and tails, but laughing and giving each other little shoves as though they were a pair of schoolboys. Their faces looked fresh and scrubbed, their damped-down curls were already springing out of place.

A moment later Mabel appeared on the landing surveying the scene below like an empress on a palace balcony. She looked like a pillar of white satin, and with her smooth, moulded arms and shoulders and her coiled golden braids

I thought I had never seen her look so fine. High on her bare arm she wore a diamond band that winked as if flashing out a message. I recognised it as the band Uncle Ben had bought her – together with so much else – when he'd taken her to Paris to launch her as a young lady. But then Evelyn spoiled the effect by nudging me and whispering, 'I think Mabel is wearing rouge!'

'She can't be,' I whispered back, shocked. Papa would have exploded with fury had he found a daughter of his resorting to cosmetics, and Aunt Barbara would also have had a thing or two to say on the subject. I remembered her description of a young lady who painted her face – 'A dreadful sight! All her natural dignity was lost.' But I couldn't help noticing that Mabel's cheeks did look suspiciously pink . . .

All accounted my party a great success. Never have I danced so much! Uncle Ben arrived, late, but full of good cheer, and he and I took a turn at dancing with everyone. I even danced with Harry and old Mr Stapleton. And I had to take a few turns with Hugh, for politeness' sake. Wouldn't it be convenient if Hugh Stapleton's attentions made my heart beat faster? But I don't think that's going to happen.

Mabel stepped out for dance after dance with Mr Glover. When they sat out, they did so together. I saw Uncle Ben watching them as they perched on a chaise longue together, eating ices and murmuring confidentially, and his face was like thunder. He stepped forward. 'High time you danced with your old uncle, young lady. Excuse me, Glover. I claim my niece.' His tone was joking, but the joke had the rumble of a threat in it, like an iceberg about to split.

And just now – I'm writing as fast as I can – just now, on the landing, when we were on our way to bed, I saw Mabel, and Mr Glover was standing very near her. Mabel tugged at the diamond band on her arm, saying it chafed her, and Mr Glover said, 'Allow me.' He unfastened it, and ran his forefinger lightly over the place where it had pressed into her soft white skin. Then he lifted her arm, turned it over, and pressed his lips to the underside of her wrist.

I stood as still as any stone, even though a feeling like a hot wave was running through me. I knew I shouldn't have seen what I saw. Luckily for me, Mabel and Mr Glover turned the other way, and I darted into my room and closed the door as softly as I could.

All of a sudden I feel quite grown up. I'm shivering now, even though I've wrapped my wolverine skin over my nightgown. I can't write much more – the candle's guttering – now it's gone. Goodnight!

Aunt Barbara
April, 1883

If Mabel were to marry Mr Glover, what would become of me?

It is selfish to ask such a question, when all I should hope for is my sister's happiness, not my own. It is strange, too, that the question has only just occurred to me. After all, it's always been 'on the cards' that Mabel will marry, if not Mr Glover, then *somebody*, because – well, that's what people do. Though I'm not sure that I ever will.

When a young lady marries, she leaves her childhood home and sets up a new home with her husband. My crusading aunts, Barbara and Nanny, would I am sure say she is under no obligation to do any such thing but that is the usual course of events. If Mabel leaves Yotes Court, would I be allowed to stay here, alone except for the servants? There's Harry, to be sure, but when he leaves Oxford in June he plans to travel out to India. When Papa lived in India, as well as being a soldier and a policeman he was tutor to a young prince, who is now a rajah, the ruler of a great province. When the rajah heard of Papa's death he wrote to Harry inviting him to his palace, so that he can honour the son of the highly respected General Ludlow.

What wouldn't I give to go too! When I think of India, I think of tigers and elephants and gorgeously coloured butterflies as wide as the palm of your hand; I think of the rajah sitting on his jewelled throne being cooled by fans made of peacock feathers, and of dancing girls with scented garlands round their necks and golden bangles jingling at their wrists. I long to see it all for myself, but Harry says it is out of the question. He says India is far too dangerous. Why, I wonder, is it safe enough for him, if it is too dangerous for me?

Oh dear, I'm wandering from the point again! Miss Kahn is right when she says that my compositions wander like bird tracks in the snow! Where was I? Oh yes, my future. Quite an important subject, really. When Harry returns from India, in the autumn, he'll start training to be an engineer. So I don't suppose he'll be at Yotes very often. And that would leave little me as head of the household! Would Uncle Ben allow it? Or would Uncle Ben come to live at Yotes with me?

Creathy is always telling me not to let my imagination run wild, and I know that's exactly what I'm doing now. What do I know about Mr Glover's intentions? I saw him place a kiss upon Mabel's bare wrist on the night of my birthday party, but that is all. One kiss is not a proposal of marriage! But I don't think I am imagining a change in Mabel's behaviour since that night. She seems more absent-minded, dreamier – except when the postman is expected, and then she's sitting bolt upright on the sofa by the window in the morning room, waiting for Louisa to bring in the letters. And I notice that my dear sister is bending the rules of mourning as far as she can. She has trimmed her black bonnet with heliotrope ribbon, and has enlivened her black cashmere with white lace at the collar and cuffs.

If Mabel were to become Mrs Arthur Glover, she might well assume that I would go with her, and make my home with them. But I wouldn't want to do that. I'm not sure that I like Mr Arthur Glover very much.

Why don't I care for him? Evelyn is not the only person who thinks him handsome. I have heard our maids whispering and giggling about him, about how tall and strong he is, and how white his teeth are. He dances well, and sings and plays tennis – in fact, he likes all the things Mabel enjoys. Are they not, then, ideally suited? But all he knows of Mabel is what I might call her party side, when she laughs and chats as if she has not a care in the world. Does Mr Glover know that sometimes she bursts into angry tears because her glove is missing a button, or speaks so sharply, when a dish has been a little underdone, that I am afraid Cook will hand in her notice? Does he know that his beloved can mope for hours on end, staring out of her bedroom window and ignoring efforts to cheer her? I wonder, would marriage cure her of her melancholy fits? Would Mabel and Mr Glover go on singing and dancing after they were married?

Perhaps it's just because I want Mabel to stay here at Yotes that I don't like Mr Glover. Though I hope there's a little more to it than that! There's something weak about him, although he is a skilful rider and an expert oarsman –

I admit I have enjoyed being rowed by him to the island in the middle of our lake, and he was brave to rescue me when I fell in. But it always seems to me that there is nothing behind that pleasing appearance and that ready smile, that the strong arms are strong to no purpose.

These are harsh words. I may be proved wrong. He and Harry arrive tomorrow, and they intend to stay for at least a week. I shall have plenty of opportunity to observe him.

Here's a surprise! My plan to watch over our visitor's every move has been, at least, delayed. We were sitting at tea yesterday, Mabel and I, when the second post brought a letter from Henrietta, Aunt Barbara's maid. Henrietta is almost as much a friend as she is a servant. 'My dear, dear Miss,' she wrote, 'I am so fritened for your pore dear Aunt. She was took Worse in that East wind and truly she needs help she does not sleep of nights but cals out for company. My dear Miss Mabel a visit from you would ese my mind.' As you can guess, Henrietta had but little schooling – indeed, it was Aunt Bar who taught her to read and write at all – but she is a good, kind soul who would lay down her life for Aunt Bar, her beloved 'Madame'.

Mabel's brow darkened as she read the letter. 'How very inconvenient. I simply cannot go to Scalands. Half the county come to play tennis here on Saturday.' Mabel had, I knew, invited two families to take part in a little tournament on Saturday afternoon, weather permitting, but I would not call that half the county. Notes of cancellation would have been little trouble. But I could see that my stubborn sister had no intention of missing even a part of Mr Glover's visit.

She tipped the cooling remains of her tea into the slop basin and poured herself a fresh cup. Her china-blue eyes gazed at me thoughtfully above the rim. 'Milicent,' she said, handing the letter to me. 'Aunt Barbara needs help. It is out of the question for me to abandon my duties as hostess, but there is no reason why you should not go in my stead.'

My feelings were mixed. I love Aunt Bar, and I hope that I will always strive to help her, but I had a strong desire to stay at Yotes and keep watch while Arthur Glover was there. And besides, I do not like it when Mabel dictates my actions, as she is inclined to do. So I said, piously, 'Oh, Mabel, are you forgetting that I have promised to take Mrs Stapleton's Sunday School class for her, until she recovers from her cold?'

'Aunt Barbara's indisposition is more important than Mrs Stapleton's sniffle,' declared Mabel in a voice that told me my fate was sealed.

I packed my paintbox and my little travelling easel, because I hoped Aunt Bar would feel well enough to give me some painting lessons. I packed my notebook too; I always need to be able to write, wherever I go. My notebook is a sketchbook too, only in it I sketch with words.

Mabel, who has grand ideas about so many things, doesn't see the point in wasting money on railway tickets, especially when it's not she who has to make the journey, so Creathy and I travelled third class. Of course Creathy came too; a young lady like me could not make even a short journey on her own.

Actually I rather like to travel third class, because one can observe different kinds of people, and if one wants to be a novelist – as I do – one needs to collect characters. On this journey from Tonbridge to Robertsbridge we sat opposite a young footman with a cold in his head who sucked peppermints noisily all the way, and a lady's maid who kept her feet firmly on her mistress's jewel case and glared at Creathy and me as if we were highwaymen.

Creathy took out her tatting – she's knotting a fringe

for the heavy cloth that covers the schoolroom piano – and I took out *Ivanhoe*, which Harry says is his favourite of Sir Walter Scott's novels. But the words wriggled off the page and floated before my eyes and I found my mind turning back to Yotes. Mr Glover and Harry would be arriving at about this time. How would Mabel greet them? With an embrace for Harry and a simple handshake for Mr Glover, as usual? Or would some secret sign pass between them? No sign would have escaped my watchful gaze, if only I had been there!

Henrietta met us at Robertsbridge station in the pony trap, and as we trotted to Scalands through the deep Sussex lanes Arthur Glover receded from my mind. The banks were studded with rosettes of primroses, the air was soft with the smell of damp moss, and the tender new leaves trembling above our head reminded me of when I was a tiny thing, riding on Papa's shoulders along these very lanes, my head among the young branches.

Arriving at Scalands always gives me a thrill. It is quite unlike any other house, just as Aunt Bar is unlike any other person. She designed the house and laid out the garden according to her own plan, and together they tell the story of her life and travels.

She wanted the house to feel simple, almost primitive, like a Saxon manor house at the time of the Battle of Hastings. The site of that great conflict of 1066 is only three or four miles from Scalands – in a town named Battle, would you believe! – and round the top of her dining-room wall is a painted frieze taken from the Bayeux Tapestry, that great stretch of embroidered storytelling fashioned by William the Conqueror's wife Queen Mathilda and her ladies, or so the legend has it.

At Scalands there is no grand entrance, no gravel sweep, no footman to take your hat and coat. You walk up the garden path of uneven rosy brick and step straight into the parlour, the floor of which is made of the same brick, so inside and outside are hardly separated. The floors are softened by woven rugs from Algiers – Aunt Barbara has a house in Algiers, right next door to Aunt Nanny and Isa, a lovely white house covered in purple bougainvillea, but since her seizure she hasn't been able to travel out there.

The parlour is furnished with low couches, covered with a rough brownish cloth that's almost like sacking, and scattered over them are cushions embroidered in the same rich reds and deep blues as the rugs on the floor. The dull plain colour of the couches makes those cushions glow like stained glass.

All round the walls are wooden shelves, painted white, which show off the pots, jars and dishes Aunt Bar has collected on her travels. She has no taste for delicate porcelain. These are thick, heavy pieces, painted with swirls and zigzags, made by peasants – on some of them you can see the thumbprints of the man or woman who worked the clay. Of earth, air, fire and water, the four elements, her favourite is earth, Aunt Barbara says.

There are paintings everywhere, but these are not formal portraits in gilt frames, or Biblical scenes painting a moral, such as we have at Yotes. They are Aunt Bar's own wild landscapes, dashed off to capture a certain light effect or a change in the weather. She's recently completed a new set of paintings – desolate Arctic scenes done from her imagination after listening to Uncle Ben recount his adventures. There's only one really big picture in the room, and that's a portrait of Aunt Bar herself made by a friend of hers, a lady artist. She's posing as Boadicea, fearless leader of the early Britons. Her red-gold hair streams in the wind and she looks every inch the warrior queen.

The portrait hangs opposite her fireplace. The bricks

that surround the fireplace have been left bare, except that they are ornamented all over with the names of Aunt Bar's visitors. Some of these are the names of people who have achieved great things. There's Mr Rossetti the painter, for instance, and Miss Blackwell, who is the first female ever to become a doctor, and Mrs Lewes, who under her pen name 'George Eliot' is a famous writer of novels. She used a man's name because she thought nobody would publish her books if they were written by a woman. The secret's out now, and Aunt Bar was the first to guess it. Papa would not let me read her novels; of course I've always wondered why, and I'm going to embark on them soon, as soon as we're out of mourning. It would have seemed disrespectful to Papa to have fallen upon them the minute he was gone.

In amongst the signatures of Aunt Bar's interesting friends are our family names, lots of them, because everybody visits Aunt Bar. Papa painted a little elephant by his name, because he used to live in India, and Cousin Amy's husband, the clever Dr Moore who tells us such funny stories about Ireland, has written his name in Irish. There's my name, too – rather wobbly. I will paint it more carefully next time. Will it be one of the famous names one day? Will people in a hundred years' time peer at it and say, 'Ah, Milicent Ludlow! That must be *the* Milicent Ludlow, the celebrated author,' I wonder.

❧ ❧ ❧

Aunt Bar was sitting in the garden when we arrived. She was in her big wickerwork chair on the terrace, swathed in a flowing cloak of a soft purplish colour. Aunt Bar won't wear stays, or corsets, and neither will Aunt Nanny nor her friend Isa. They say they deform the body. Their clothes are loose fitting and fluid. Aunt Jenny says they don't look respectable and she always makes Roddy wear tight-laced stays; I expect she was the same with Amy, before she married. Mabel wears stays when she dresses up, because she likes to give the appearance of having a small waist and an impressive bosom – Mabel might not like me to write that, but it's true. But when she's just messing about at home, bathing the dogs or cutting flowers or sketching out of doors, she leaves her stays off, and then she looks less elegant but more approachable.

Aunt Bar doesn't like the bright artificial dyes that are all the rage nowadays. She only wears fabric coloured with old-fashioned vegetable dyes, in gentle shades of green and blue and purple. When we arrived and I saw her sitting there on the terrace, I thought how the colour of her cloak echoed the colour of the distant hills, and I thought about how in Aunt Barbara's life everything flows in and out of nature. In her house every table top bears a posy of wild flowers, or an arrangement of twigs, leaves, seashells, stones, even birds' nests. In her garden she does not plant flowers, as most gardeners do, in geometrical lines and blocks of colour. At Yotes the parterre is laid out in a symmetrical pattern based on one of Papa's Indian prints, and I remember how Aunt Bar hurt Papa's feelings by saying that it was 'like some vulgar carpet'. She did not mean to offend, I'm sure, but she cannot help but speak her mind. At Scalands the flowers are released from their corsets. In summer, clematis and honeysuckle scramble through the trees and the front of the house is smothered in sweet-smelling yellow roses. Now, on a clear spring day, Creathy and I admired the drifts of white narcissi dotted with brownish-purple snake's head fritillaries that peeped through the long grass and blended with the wild woodland that fringed the garden.

Aunt Bar rose to her feet and held out her arms when she saw us, but before I could hug her she had to grip the arm of her chair. 'Welcome, little elf-child!' she cried as she held me by the chin and scanned my face for signs of ill-health. All the aunts do this, whenever a nephew or a niece comes within their orbit.

'A little pale,' was her verdict, 'and still thin, but your eyes are bright. Henrietta, we'll have luncheon here on the terrace, if you would be so kind. Why should we waste one drop of this glorious sunshine? Now sit down, child, and tell me everything. What have you been reading, what has Miss Kahn been teaching you? Tell me all about Mabel and Harry, and whether there are any piglets in your styes, and whether Scray has had any more puppies. Do not leave anything out.'

We sat in the sun and ate new bread and pressed beef and radishes and cheese, and a gooseberry jam tart with thick yellow cream, and between mouthfuls I tried to answer my aunt's questions, but each answer provoked a hail of fresh enquiries, until Henrietta said, 'Madame, have mercy on the poor child, she'll choke!' Henrietta sat down and ate with us. Aunt Jenny disapproved of Aunt Bar's habit of treating servants as friends – she thinks it makes them 'uppity'. But I like Henrietta to sit with us, because she is always kind; she made the most beautiful little pink quilted bedjacket for me when I was ill with whooping cough. Henrietta is very tall, as tall as a man. Aunt Bar had the legs of the dining-room sideboard made longer so that Henrietta wouldn't crick her back when she served the food.

When we had eaten our fill – and I ate a great deal more than I do at home, where the schoolroom luncheon nearly always seems to be boiled mutton and rice pudding – Henrietta asked, 'Madame, will you take your rest now?' But Aunt Bar stoutly replied, 'No rest for me today, Henrietta. Creathy shall take my rest in my stead. *I* am going to make the most of Milicent. Fetch your painting things, child, for I am sure you have brought them with you, and we will sit in the sun and make pictures and talk about everything in Heaven and Earth and a good deal besides.'

I carried the easels and paintboxes to a spot at the end of the garden where the distant view, flanked by woodland on both sides, is framed by the towering jawbone of a whale. Uncle Ben brought this back from the Arctic, on his first expedition I believe. The jawbone is strangely delicate in appearance, shaped like a curving version of a capital A without the central bar. It has a holy look, I think, as if it were the doorway to a cathedral. When I told Aunt Barbara this she pointed to the fields and hills beyond and said, 'You are right, because there is my cathedral.'

We gazed in silence at the misty blue distance. I listened to the weak bleats of new lambs and the deeper calls of their mothers from the farm in the valley below us, and as I listened I became aware of another sound. Aunt Bar's breathing was laboured now. I must have given her an anxious look, for she smiled, patted her chest, and said, 'I sound as if I am harbouring a family of frogs in here. They don't hurt me, but they do slow me down rather.'

She gave me a few pieces of advice before we began to paint – choose a focal point to draw the eye into the picture; apply colour quickly and boldly, don't try to correct what you have done or the picture will lose its 'snap'. Then she began on her own painting. Her hand is no longer steady, but she has turned this to her advantage. Her wavery brushmarks are more fluid now, more natural because less precise. Within minutes she had set down a living, breathing landscape. I tried to copy her, and produced only a series of smudges.

'Tell me,' she said when she had set my sketch to rights. 'What is your opinion of Mr Arthur Glover?'

I was startled. I thought nobody outside Yotes Court

knew anything about Arthur Glover, except perhaps, vaguely, that he was an Oxford friend of Harry's. I felt myself blush, and Aunt Bar smiled.

'I thought as much. I had heard a little rumour from a certain quarter, and that pretty colour in your cheeks confirms what I had heard. Well, my dear, don't answer my question if it makes you feel uncomfortable.'

It came to me in a flash that the 'certain quarter' must be Henrietta, who was great friends with our maid Louisa. Servants are very good at noticing things. Before I could think carefully about whether or how I should answer Aunt Barbara's question, I found myself blurting out, 'Oh, Aunt, I don't want Mr Glover to marry Mabel!'

Aunt Bar laid aside her paintbrush and placed her hand over mine. I could feel the tremor in it as she gave me a little squeeze. 'Think carefully, my child. Could it be that you would rather nobody married Mabel? Could it be that you want her all to yourself?'

'I cannot answer that question,' I said, sounding prim when I meant to sound thoughtful, 'until I have given it some serious thought. I will give you your answer tonight.'

105

For the rest of the day I was never alone with Aunt Barbara, so I had no opportunity to discuss Arthur Glover. My aunt seemed much more vigorous and less of an invalid than Henrietta's letter had led me to expect, and I heard Creathy express this opinion too, when she though she was out of earshot. 'She's not so bad by day, Mrs MacCreath,' explained Henrietta, 'and she's bucked up by Miss Milicent being here, but her nights are terrible. All her fears come crowding in upon her. I sit up with her, and tend to the fire, but what she wants is a body to read aloud to her, to take her mind off things. Ever since her seizure, she's been troubled with her imaginings. But as you know, Mrs MacCreath, I'm not much of a scholar.'

I know I wasn't supposed to be listening to this conversation, which was taking place in the kitchen with the door open, but I couldn't help butting in. 'I'll read to her, Creathy,' I said, popping my head round the door. 'You know how she loves to hear me read.' But Creathy said, as I knew she would, 'Miss Milicent, if you think I'm going to let you stop up half the night with your weak chest, you've got another think coming.' She laid a hand on Henrietta's arm. 'Don't you worry, I'll get up and read to her. I'll leave my chamber door ajar so that I can hear

106

her bell. You make sure you get a proper night's rest, Henrietta. You'll need all your strength.'

That night, after Creathy tucked me up in bed she closed the door firmly behind her. But as soon as she had gone I sat up and pressed my head against the cold brass bed rail so that I wouldn't drift off to sleep. I would know when Creathy was asleep – her room was across the landing from mine, and I was certain to hear her snores. Creathy usually snored, especially when she had been imbibing 'the creater' as she called Scotch whisky, and that evening Aunt Bar had been insistent that she sample some.

I was right – it didn't take long. I'm sorry if I sound indelicate, but Creathy snores like our old Berkshire sow! I'm rather fond of the sound, actually, because I've known it all my life. Once her snores had established a rhythm, I crept out of bed, and opened my door as wide as it would go.

I must have dozed off after all, for the sound of Aunt Bar's bell entered a dream I was having about Mabel's wedding and turned itself into the sound of the church bell. I was glad to be woken because it wasn't a very nice dream. Mabel was wearing a big white veil, but when her groom raised it, he discovered a face that was cracked and eyeless,

107

like a broken china doll. At first I thought the groom was Mr Glover, but then somehow he turned into Uncle Ben. He seized the doll-Mabel and shook her, and the bell rang, and I jumped out of bed, bundled my shawl about me, and padded down the corridor to Aunt Barbara.

Lit only by the dying fire she looked iller than she did in daylight. Her hair hung down on either side of her head in snaky ropes; the shadows carved hollows into her face and turned her eyes into black pools. Her voice, too, was different; hoarse, and gasping. I would have been frightened, if I had been of nervous disposition like, say, cousin Roddy, but I am not easily frightened. 'Henrietta,' Aunt Barbara croaked, 'my pillows have slipped – I cannot breathe.'

'It's not Henrietta, Aunt Bar,' I whispered, plumping up her pillows and helping her to shift position. I already knew that since her seizure she was not allowed to lie flat. 'My little elf-child,' she murmured. 'How good you are.'

I made up the fire, lit a candle and set it beside the bed, feeling as I did so like our famous cousin Florence Nightingale. Then I climbed into bed next to my aunt, which is *not* the sort of thing Miss Nightingale would have done! The bed was a big wooden one, both ends carved into wave shapes, like a grand sledge. The story was that Aunt Bar had loved sleeping in just such a bed in France, and when a fine old cherry tree had fallen in Scalands Wood she had asked the village carpenter to use the cherry wood to make a replica of it – she drew it from memory, and gave the carpenter her drawings to use. There was plenty of room in it for me. 'Heavens, child!' my aunt exclaimed. 'Your feet are like blocks of ice!'

I rolled my feet in the hem of my nightgown. 'Aunt Bar,' I said. 'You asked me a question about Mabel, and I said I would give you an answer. I think the best answer I could give would be to tell you about my dream.' And I described it to her – the lifted veil, the shattered face, the empty eyes. But for some reason I left out the part about Uncle Ben.

My aunt listened with close attention. 'My dear,' she said at last, 'marriage is not the glorious solution to life's problems that so many girls hope and believe it to be. Young as you are, I think you may already have realised that. But Mabel, I fear, is the kind of girl who will jump at any chance of marriage, and it would be quite wrong to attempt to prevent her. So we may indeed soon find that Mr Glover is to be a member of our family. Let us think of what we know about him that is to his credit.'

'Well,' said I, 'he is a friend of Harry's.'

'That's one good thing. Tell me another.'

'I've heard him praised as a brave rider-to-hounds.'

'Physical courage is not to be sniffed at. Anything else?'

I pondered for a while. 'He plays and sings tolerably well, I suppose,' was all I came up with. 'And – and there's tennis.'

Aunt Bar laughed. 'Ah, tennis! Tennis is very important. We will not list any faults we may suspect, certainly not in the middle of the night, when thoughts tend towards gloom. Do you think you could read aloud to me, my dear? I find that is the best way of banishing troubles.'

I picked up the book that was lying next to the bed. It was a volume of old ballads. I am afraid I read but stumblingly, for the old-fashioned words confused me, and the stories were so sad, I worried they would alarm my aunt.

'The stalk is wither'd and dry, sweetheart,

And the flower will never return;

And since I lost my own sweetheart,

What can I do but mourn?'

How could such words lull anyone to sleep? And yet the rhymes and the cadences seemed to soothe her. As for me, I was entranced by the tales of broken hearts and cruel murders, of nut-brown maidens and talking crows, of milk-white steeds and dungeons deep and the Queen o' the Fairies, and I continued to read long after she had fallen asleep.

Little Hatty Nicolls
June, 1883

I am feeling most peculiar today, but whether that's because I am 'coming down with something', as Creathy would say, or whether it's because of the events of this morning, who can tell?

In any case, our household has been feeling a little mournful lately, because we have said goodbye to Harry. True to his word, no sooner had he completed his final term at Oxford, than he packed up and set off for India. He will return in September, in three months' time, or a little more. That isn't really such a long absence. When he was boarding at Rugby School he would often be away for three months at a stretch. But India is so far away . . . I don't let myself imagine man-eating tigers and tropical diseases, because I know Harry himself refuses to think about such things.

Mabel, Creathy and I travelled to Southampton to see him off. The ship he sailed in was huge, like a floating city. They 'get up' dances on deck, and concerts and amateur theatricals. Harry says the voyage will be one long party. They stop for a day or two at Port Said, and Harry says he will write to us from there and tell us of the wonders he has seen. I hope he doesn't forget. He looked so jaunty and carefree, with his curly hair and the new little moustache he's so proud of. He waved his handkerchief to us until the last possible moment, and when the ship at last eased out of sight, I must confess that both Mabel and I shed tears.

That was nearly a week ago. Now life at Yotes has settled down into a humdrum routine, but we keep giving ourselves little treats to take our minds off Harry. Yesterday, Mabel ordered melon from the hothouse, and the first picking of strawberries, to enliven our luncheon. Then we fairly gorged ourselves. Could the melon account for my faint feelings of sickness? Papa was always of the opinion that too much fruit was inadvisable.

In the afternoon, Mabel and I paid a visit to the Lodge

cottage that stands at the end of our avenue, to enquire after little Hatty Nicolls, the lodge-keeper's daughter, who has a fever. Our cook made a sponge cake for her, and we took that in a basket, together with a few strawberries, because her mother, poor thing, is trying to tempt her appetite. I brought a paintbox too, because that might encourage her to get well. I know she will love to use it. Miss Kahn thought we should not go, for fear of catching her malady, but Mabel said, 'Papa would have wanted it,' so that was that. Mabel likes to make a point of being brave. But *would* Papa have wanted us to go? He always urged us to do our duty, but he had a dread of our catching diseases – not surprising when you remember what happened to my poor brother Edmund, the brother I never saw.

Poor little Hatty was lying very flat in her truckle bed. Only her head and hands emerged from the faded patchwork quilt, but I could see by her wrists how pitifully thin she had become. Her pinched face was very white; her pretty fair hair was dark with moisture, and stuck to her forehead in stripes. By her side, Mabel's round pink cheeks and thick shiny hair looked like an affront.

Hatty smiled when she saw what we had brought her, but she could only whisper her thanks. 'Won't you try a crumb of cake, my dear?' her mother urged, but Hatty feebly shook her head and put her hand to her throat.

'She can't swallow aught,' said her mother, apologising for what looked like a rejection of our gift. 'She'll take some presently, I'll be bound.'

'What does the doctor say?' asked Mabel. Mrs Nicolls looked embarrassed. 'We haven't . . .' Her sentence trailed away, and Mabel and I exchanged a glance as we both realised there was no money to pay the doctor. I looked back at Hatty, who looked so tiny and so fragile that I could not resist bending over her and placing a kiss on her damp forehead. 'Miss Milicent!' said her mother, shooing me away. 'You didn't ought to be doing that!' But she looked a little pleased, all the same.

The lodge cottage is only half a mile from Yotes, but the walk back seemed hot and laborious in the June sun. I was not much inclined for conversation, but I did say, 'Do you think we should tell Doctor Hooker to call on them?' and Mabel agreed. As soon as we reached home, she sent Sam, our young manservant, with a summons to the doctor. 'Bid him present the bill to me,' I heard her say.

The hot walk made my head ache, and Mabel was so kind and sympathetic. She made me lie on the drawing-room sofa with a damp muslin folded on my forehead, and she herself went to the pantry to fetch me a glass of cool ginger beer.

Well, that was yesterday. Today is another story. I feel giddy and shaky, and there's a tight, pulling feeling at the back of my throat. Evelyn is expected to tea, and she is bringing little Frank, who always cheers me up. She's also bringing her diary, which she says is a secret from everyone in the world except me, and she's going to let me read it! But for the first time in my life, I don't want to see her. And I don't believe I could eat my tea, either, even though I know that Cook has made the sticky dark treacle cake that is Evelyn's favourite. All I want to do is crawl into a hole and suffer alone, like a wounded fox.

I am very, very upset – more upset than I've ever been, except I suppose when somebody has died. I don't ever remember feeling so shaky before. Have I caught the malady from Hatty Nicolls, or could the events of this morning have produced this physical effect?

Painful though it is to do so, I will now relate what happened. Miss Kahn woke with a severe headache, so Evelyn and I were excused lessons – which was why Evelyn was asked to tea instead – and, as Wednesday is Creathy's

116

day for Maidstone market, Mabel and I were alone. We decided to paint in the morning room. Mabel set a brown earthenware jug of ox-eye daisies on the piano, which is the sort of subject Aunt Barbara likes. We sat sketching away quite companionably. Mabel's painting style is rather hard and angular – she is over-fond of definite outlines – so I was explaining to her about Aunt Bar's practice of dashing the colours, very wet, onto paper to achieve that fluid, natural appearance, and Mabel was quarrelling mildly about it and telling me I was too young to be instructing my big sister, but it was a gentle tease.

Then in came Louisa with a letter on the silver tray. She presented it, not to Mabel as I would have expected, but to me; then she withdrew. It was addressed to 'Miss M. Ludlow', but I did not recognise the handwriting. I slit the envelope with a little silver knife that Mama used to sharpen her drawing pencils, and which I now use for the same purpose, and drew out the letter.

'My dearest,' I read, 'I think about you day and night –' I must have changed colour, for Mabel leapt to her feet and grabbed the envelope from my lap. 'Give me that!' she shrieked. I clung to the letter. It was addressed to me, and besides, I objected to being ordered about in that way.

I read on. 'Your beauty dazzles me, the touch of your sweet lips is –' But I never reached the end of that sentence, for Mabel seized my wrist and twisted it in an attempt to force the letter from my grasp.

Still I would not give in. 'You have no business –' I protested, but my protest was swiftly drowned, as Mabel lunged for the jug of daisies and dashed its contents over my head.

There I sat, gasping, dripping and speechless. The precious letter was soaked. Mabel took it from my now limp hand and attempted to limit the damage by blotting it with her handkerchief. 'You little sneak!' she hissed. 'I'll never forgive you for this – never!' The venom in her voice made me tremble, but with rage, not with fear. I swept my painting things together – my daisy sketch was ruined, which was a pity, as it had been going rather well – and shaking the broken flowers from my clothing and hair I stalked from the room without another word.

I took myself off to the rose garden, hoping to avoid seeing anyone in my bedraggled state. I sat on the teak bench in the sun, to dry my hair and clothes, but despite the warmth of the day I could not prevent my shivers. I tried to think of far-away things – I stroked the smooth bench with my fingertips, forcing myself to imagine the dark dense jungle where the tree from which it was made had grown, picturing the strings of ants with their powerful jaws which had tried in vain to make their way through its iron hardness. I closed my eyes and tried to hear the howling and whooping of the monkeys and the shrieks of brilliantly coloured birds . . . but my mind would keep coming back to the here and now, to the worst argument I had ever had with my only sister.

Had I been at fault? Louisa had presented the letter to me, so of course I had taken it. Why had Mr Glover – for of course he was the writer, though I had not had time to see the signature – why had he addressed it to 'Miss M. Ludlow' instead of simply 'Miss Ludlow', which would have been the correct way to style Mabel, as the oldest sister. Mabel had trained Louisa a little too well!

Mr Stapleton, when preparing Evelyn and me for confirmation, had always urged us to scrutinise our consciences in the minutest detail. If I am quite truthful, I admit that I had realised, very soon, that the letter could not have been for me. Who do I know who 'thinks about me day and night'? I should have handed it straight to Mabel. Of course I should. But why, oh why, could she not have asked for it politely? Why did she resort first to commands, then to violence, when a single gentle sentence would have achieved the end she desired?

The bees boomed in the lavender hedges that framed the rose garden, the white fantail doves crooned as they popped in and out of the little windows in their dovecot, the sun's heat caused the clove pinks and the gilly flowers to pour their spicy odours into the summer air. Weekes, our head gardener, passed by with a trug full of fresh-picked strawberries. He stopped, tipped his hat to me, and without appearing to notice my still-damp and dishevelled condition, he invited me to taste. I gave him what I hoped was a fair imitation of my usual smile, but my heart was thumping so hard that I thought it must be visible through my clothes. The sweet juice stung my throat; I could hardly swallow. I sniffed my fingers. Usually, the jammy smell of strawberries on my fingers is delightful to me, but today it brought me no solace.

I felt dizzy – so dizzy. I bade Weekes good morning, and made my way slowly back to the house. As I pushed open the heavy front door, Mabel pulled it from within with such violence that I nearly tumbled headlong into the hall. One glance at her face told me that I was not forgiven;

her mouth was a thin straight line. 'There you are!' she exclaimed, and her voice had not lost its poisonous hiss. 'What do you mean by running off like that? Go straight to your room and stay there until you can apologise!'

Usually I would have fought against such an unfair command, but I felt so dizzy that I obeyed without a word. So here I am now, lying on my bed, writing in pencil because I have been in trouble for spilling ink on the bedclothes more times than I care to remember. My pinafore is still damp, and I know I should have taken it off, but I just don't have the strength. It was all I could do to unhook the buttons on my boots.

It feels most unnatural to be lying fully clothed on my bed in the middle of a beautiful June day, wishing with all my heart that my dearest friend was not coming to tea. When I close my eyes, hot tears slide out and I seem unable to prevent them. I want Creathy to come back from the market. She's the only person I want to see.

The Tolling of the Bell
August, 1883

Well! Wherever was I?

I have been ill – very ill. When I reread what I last wrote, a lifetime ago in June, I can see it in my handwriting. It looks like the handwriting of somebody who is deranged, or dying, or both! Now here I am sitting at a writing table in my comfortable bedroom at this inn on the Isle of Wight, and before me is a view of the sparkling sea with white sails bobbing up and down upon it. My body is still tingling from the salt bath I took earlier, and though I've been ordered to rest by Aunt Nanny, I feel no need of rest. How different the world looks now!

When Creathy returned from the Maidstone market that

fateful June day, she took one look at me huddled on my bed and sent Sam, our page boy, to the rectory with a note for Mrs Stapleton to say on no account were Evelyn and Frank to come to tea. She ordered me to undress, though it was the middle of the day, and as I did so I could hear her clucking under her breath about the marks the flower-water had left on my clothes, but I didn't get a proper scolding, which proved that she considered me to be truly ill. I crawled into bed but I couldn't get warm, despite the heat of the day. Then the shivering turned to burning, and I tried to throw the blankets off, but Creathy wouldn't let me, and I felt too weak to argue. My throat grew tighter and tighter until I could hardly speak or swallow.

Mabel came in. 'I've sent for Dr Hooker,' she announced. She laid the palm of her hand, quite tenderly, on my hot forehead. 'We should never have paid that visit to Hatty Nicolls,' she said. 'It was my fault, Creathy. Miss Kahn said we should not, but I disregarded her. The blame is mine.' In a funny way I think Mabel was glad that I was ill, because it meant our quarrel could be forgotten. It also meant that she could call for the doctor and take responsibility; she could be seen to be brave and strong. Mr Stapleton would say that we must beware of criticising others, but I don't mean that to sound like a criticism, not quite. How difficult it is to say exactly what one means!

After that, the days hardly existed for me. I was weighed down by the most immense weariness. Raising my hand to push my hair out of my eyes felt like lifting a dumb-bell, in the manner of a strongman at a fair. But swallowing was the worst thing. It was as if a hobgoblin had spun a skein across my throat, fine as a cobweb but strong as steel. I couldn't manage food at all. Creathy, Mabel, Louisa, Dr Hooker and an unfamiliar woman who I later realised was a hired nurse – they all took it in turns to urge me to sip beef tea, port wine and chicken broth. There was a little white china jug with a narrow spout, which was supposed to make drinking easier, but when they put it to my lips I spluttered and choked and the contents splashed over my sheets and nightgown. It was Mabel who had the great idea. She went out to the stables and came back with a handful of hollow straws, and I sucked up liquid through them and found I could take a little that way. Could Mabel have saved my life?

Dr Hooker came every day, sometimes twice. Even as I lay too weak to move, I thought how unjust it was that poor little Hatty Nicolls in the Lodge cottage had to rely on our charity, whereas we in the big house could summon the doctor as often as we liked. Dr Hooker sat beside my bed with his gold-rimmed pince-nez quivering on the very end of his sharp nose, and felt my neck with his chilly fingers. I knew what he was feeling for. I had diphtheria, you see, the same disease my brother Edmund died of. If you have diphtheria and the glands in your neck swell up, that is a very bad sign. The glands swell and block your air passages, and unless you are very lucky, you suffocate.

People thought that because I could hardly speak, I couldn't hear or understand. But I could. Indeed, my sense of hearing became more acute. After each visit, Dr Hooker would make his progress report to Creathy standing in the corridor outside my room, and though he closed the door I could hear every word. That's how I knew that he was watching for swellings in my neck. If they occurred, his only course of action would be to drill an air hole into my throat, which might save me. Or might not. I gave no sign that I had heard this. I lay still, and thought about the early Christian martyrs.

I learned that I was not the only invalid. That bad headache of Miss Kahn's on the morning of my fight with Mabel turned out to be the start of diphtheria for her too.

Miss Kahn recovered more quickly than I. The younger you are, the worse it is – that's the rule. But it's not an unbreakable rule. One of the Queen's grown-up daughters died of it – Princess Alice. That was a few years ago. I had been young enough to be surprised by that. I had thought, then, that being a princess would save you from such a fate.

Little Frank Stapleton was another victim. They lowered their voices when they talked about him, but I could still hear. I think finding out that Frank was ill was the worst moment of all. I kept remembering what Frank had said to me after Papa's operation: 'If you are ever old and lost, I will look after you.' Would Frank ever grow old himself, now? Or would he be lost – lost to us, though not to God. I didn't try to ask for news of Frank, or of Hatty. I could barely whisper, and besides, I knew they wouldn't tell me.

I didn't really *do* anything while I was ill. The light hurt my eyes, so my curtains were kept closed. Mabel said she would read to me, but Dr Hooker said, 'No, she must have absolute rest.' Strangely enough, I wasn't bored. If I had been well I would have been bored to screaming point and beyond, but for me time had disappeared; the ticking of the clock on the mantelshelf blended with the beating of my heart, and I felt almost as if I was floating. All the normal everyday things seemed to drift away. Sometimes I thought, I wonder if I am already dead? But then Creathy would come in with a big black medicine bottle, or I would hear the maids banging their brooms in the corridor, and I would realise that Death hadn't come for me just yet.

One day, a very still warm day, Louisa came in to open my windows. The doctor had decreed that they should remain closed except for a ten-minute period once a day, when they were opened to let the bad air out. Extra covers were put over me while the windows were open, for fear of a chill, though how you catch a chill on a hot summer's day, even if you are ill, I did not understand. As I lay pinned under the pile of quilts and blankets, like the princess and the pea in reverse, listening to the never-ending tick of the clock and the swishing sounds Louisa made as she tidied the room, I became aware of another sound. I heard the church bell, not ringing out in a peal as it did on Sundays and holy days, but tolling, slow, steady and sad. The notes of the bell seemed to hang in the air like round, dark, solid *things*. How can a sound be a *thing*? It's nonsense, but it seemed like sense to me.

'Louisa,' I whispered, and she started, for I hardly spoke at all. 'Louisa, are they tolling the bell for me?'

'Bless you, no, Miss Milicent! That bell's for –' but then Louisa clapped her hand over her mouth. 'You're not to talk,' she said. 'And gloomy thoughts is bad for you.' She closed the windows and left the room.

Later, Mabel came in. She looked at me, and must have decided I was asleep, for she said nothing to me, but knelt down by the side of my bed, and put her hands together in a prayer. To my surprise, she prayed aloud. 'O Lord,' I heard her say, 'take Hatty Nicolls into Thy eternal care. Comfort her parents in their distress. Dear Lord, I beseech Thee, spare my sister Milicent. Lord, lift the curse my mother laid on me.' She paused, and I thought I heard a muffled sob. 'Dear Lord, if Thou wilt spare my only sister, I'll do anything You like, really I will. I will never think or speak badly about anyone again. Dear Lord, who already hast Edmund in Thy keeping, don't take my sister too. Let me keep my sister, and I'll – yes, I'll even give *him* up, if such is Thy will.'

I understood at once that Mabel was offering to give up Arthur Glover if that would save my life. I also understood, somehow, that the prayer was more to me than to God.

But strange to say, it was not until my illness was passed that I remembered the tolling bell, and knew that it had rung for the funeral of Hatty Nicolls.

❧ ❧ ❧

One morning, very early, I awoke, and knew that I was better. Through the chinks in the curtains I could guess that a beautiful dawn was breaking. Suddenly, I wanted to see the sky. I got out of bed, but I had not realised how weak I had become, and I stumbled and fell. Creathy was sleeping on the truckle bed in the corner, as she had done throughout my illness. She woke at the sound of my fall, lifted me bodily and stowed me away under the blankets again. I protested that I was quite well, and she protested that I wasn't. When she heard my voice again, almost back to normal, tears of gladness stood in her eyes.

The days of my convalescence were enjoyable at first. I was propped up in bed on a mountain of pillows. I nibbled thin, crustless bread and butter and sipped sweet tea. Evelyn Stapleton was allowed to visit me. She brought the happy tidings that little Frank had pulled through, and was sitting up and asking for his toys. Evelyn had told her mother that she would read aloud to me from *The Pilgrim's Progress*, but in her bag she had concealed her diary, which she had intended to show me on the day I became ill. She held the diary inside the covers of *The Pilgrim's Progress* and read bits out loud. It was full of wicked observations about everyone we knew; I laughed and laughed, which made my throat hurt again, though it made the rest of me feel better. Miss Kahn came in and asked what we were reading. Evelyn closed the book and held it up for her to see. 'Ach – so?' said Miss Kahn, puzzled. 'I know of zees book *The Pilgrim's Progress*, but I did not know it was so droll. I must read it for myself.' This made us want to laugh again. We tried not to seem rude, but it was a relief when Miss Kahn left, and we could splutter to our hearts' content. For a clergyman's daughter, Evelyn is a bold bad girl, and I told her as much!

I had been meaning to ask her about Hatty, but the laughter and the happy news of Frank, and the sight of dear Miss Kahn fully recovered, put her out of my mind. However, when Evelyn rose to go, I took her hand and said, 'Just one thing. What became of Hatty Nicolls?' Evelyn looked at me, and her merry eyes became grave. She pressed my hand, and gave a tiny shake of her head, and said nothing. I understood. The door closed behind

Evelyn, and that was when I remembered the tolling bell. I lay rigid and clenched my fists, and made a solemn vow that when I was grown up and could choose what I would do, I would work to help poor people. I didn't know how, but I would do *something*, so that people like the Nicolls could afford doctors and nurses and medicine when they fell sick. I didn't tell anyone else about my vow. I'm telling you now. Have I kept it?

A letter from Harry arrived, just when I was getting better. It was written at Port Said, as he'd promised. Hurrah! He told of flying fish like smooth white birds skimming over the Red Sea (which isn't red at all), of riding a donkey named Gladstone after our prime minister, of intolerable heat, of clever cockroaches on board ship, which evaded every shoe or book thrown at them. 'There is a single lady on board,' he wrote, 'who is travelling out to India to study and paint its plant life. This lady intends to travel the length and breadth of the country with no more protection than a furled umbrella! From the unusual design of her sun-bonnet I knew straight away that she *must* be a friend of Aunt Barbara's, and sure enough, so she proved to be!

She has shown me her sketchbook; there is even a painting of the garden at Scalands in it, with the tulip tree "large as life and twice as natural", as Creathy would say! I will write again when we reach Bombay. I think of you sitting on the lawn under the cedar sipping lemonade, and I wish I was with you. Give the dogs a pat from me.'

After a few days, the novelty of convalescent life wore off, and troubles and annoyances seemed to crowd in on me. I wanted to get up, but when I tried, my legs still buckled under me. I asked for my sketchbook – pencil only, of course, in bed – but my fingers felt nerveless, and the marks I made were feeble. I tried to read, but the sentences marched away into the distance leaving me behind. Worst of all, the kindnesses done to me seemed irritating and interfering, and I was cross and snappish with everyone.

One day, a new visitor appeared by my bedside. It was Dr Moore, the clever London doctor. I was pleased to see him, because I assumed it meant that Amy had come too, and it was always exciting to see beautiful Amy. But Dr Moore told me that Amy had gone to visit her parents at

Crowham. My face must have fallen, for he laughed, and said, 'You'll have to make do with me, young lady!'

Dr Moore explained that he had come as a doctor, not just as a visitor. He said Mabel had written to Amy, worried that I was not getting well fast enough, so he had come to find out why. He examined me carefully, looking at my tongue and into my ears. He took my pulse and my temperature, and placed his stethoscope on my chest and back. He even left a jar with me, and asked me – I'm embarrassed to write this – to 'make water' into it, when he had left the room, and he took it away to analyse it. How indelicate! But I didn't mind, too much. Dr Moore's fair beard looked soft, and smelled faintly of scented soap. His hands were warm and gentle, and his twinkly Irish eyes creased at the corners in a way I couldn't help liking. While he examined me he told me about an Irish cottager who kept a leprechaun for a year and a day, and I could almost see the little creature's feet dancing on the green turf.

When he had finished, he asked me how I passed my days. I complained, I'm afraid, about how uncomfortable I felt, and how people were always fussing over me, changing my nightgown and tugging combs through my hair and trying to make me eat and sponging me with soap that felt sticky. I told him about the medicine Dr Hooker gave me, that made me feel sick. When I had finished complaining, Dr Moore patted my hand. 'All you want,' he said, 'is to be left alone.'

Mabel came in, without knocking. 'Milicent is almost strong now,' he told her, 'but she needs a change of scene. So do you, Mabel my dear. You have been a most valiant nurse and sister, and you deserve a holiday. I prescribe sea breezes for you both.' I thought that this was a very nice kind of doctoring. I knew, from the whispers of the servants, that Uncle Willy and Aunt Jenny hadn't wanted Amy to marry Dr Moore. He was poor, and Irish, and had 'no family'. I imagine they had hoped that their attractive eldest daughter would make what is called an advantageous match. But I thought to myself, the real advantage was to marry someone who was kind and clever and did good in the world.

When Dr Moore took his leave, he picked up the big black medicine bottle and examined the label. 'You won't be needing this any more,' he said, and he took it away with him. I don't suppose I'll ever marry, but if I do, I hope my husband will have eyes that twinkle like Dr Moore's.

Mabel began planning our holiday right away. Uncle Ben was consulted. It turned out that he had already organised a sailing holiday for himself on the Isle of Wight in early August, so it seemed sensible that we should join in, though I, for one, would have to be a landlubber. Aunt Nanny had arrived from Algiers with dear Isa – they always spend the summer in England – and she proposed herself as the female leader of the party. Even Mabel didn't dare object, because Aunt Nanny is quite terrifying when she is crossed.

I make a point of *not* being afraid of Aunt Nanny. She has a sharp tongue, to be sure, but she can be very kind. She wrote me a great many letters during my illness. I didn't see them until I was better, but then I was touched to find out how worried she'd been. She and Isa travelled through Europe before their arrival in England. They were quite adventurous, scaling Swiss mountains and sailing down German rivers. In one letter Nanny drew me a picture of herself and Isa in 'rational' travelling costume of their own design – large white blouses and knee-breeches like a man's, with thick stockings and stout boots. Many people would consider it indecent to see a woman in trousers, but I agree with Aunt Nanny – what is the point of hampering yourself with skirts and petticoats if your aim is to climb a mountain? The picture was a comic one, with Nanny all long and bony in her breeches, like a flamingo, and Isa short and round, like a cottage loaf.

Once I was well enough to travel, we left Creathy at Yotes to manage what was left of the household, and set off for London – just Mabel and I, very daring! We were to spend a few days at Uncle Ben's house in Gower Street, where we would meet Aunt Nanny and do some necessary shopping.

When we arrived at Charing Cross station, who do you think hove into sight? None other than Arthur Glover! 'Forgive me,' he said, bowing and smiling – or smirking, as I would call it. 'I heard that you would be coming, and I took the liberty – here, let me find you a porter.' He stuck two fingers in his mouth and gave a shrill whistle. A porter appeared as if conjured out of thin air, and collected our luggage. I glanced furtively at Mabel, who had turned pink. She behaved as if the arrival of Mr Glover was a complete surprise, but somehow I don't think it was.

Uncle Ben's carriage was waiting in the station forecourt, and Uncle Ben himself was just coming to look for us. My dear uncle's brows always beetle, but I thought they beetled a little more than usual when he caught sight of our escort. However, the two men shook hands cordially enough, and we conversed, briefly, about the Isle of Wight. Mr Glover announced that he intended to visit cousins at Southampton very soon. 'Oh, indeed?' asked Mabel. 'Then you must come over to the Island and pay us a visit. Isn't that a good idea, Uncle Ben?'

Before Uncle Ben had time to reply, Mr Glover thanked him warmly for the invitation he had not issued, doffed his hat to us, and set off in the direction of Trafalgar Square. Just before he turned the corner out of sight he looked back, and raised his hand. Uncle Ben's back was turned, but Mabel fluttered her white handkerchief with the quickest and most discreet of movements.

Sixty-four Gower Street is a very masculine house. There isn't much furniture, and what there is is hard and uncomfortable. The cosiest spot is on the polar-bear skin rug in front of the fire in Uncle Ben's study, especially if Bob comes and presses his woolly self up against you. We were overjoyed to see Bob again, Mabel and I.

The study is an interesting room. There are framed maps on the wall with Uncle Ben's voyages marked in red.

There are portfolios of extraordinary photographs from the Arctic regions. One shows a walrus being skinned. I look at that with a mixture of horror and pity – and wonder. The walrus's skin, stretched out, is simply immense, like an expanse of rippling water.

Aunt Nanny and Isa soon joined us at Gower Street, bringing such heaps of things for me, I'm afraid Mabel was quite jealous! They brought armfuls of flowers too. 'This house is like a tomb, Ben!' Nanny declared, 'There's no colour in it.' She set vases of irises, lilies, roses and peonies in every nook and cranny, to Ben's pretended disgust.

After a few days buying summer hats and parasols and bathing equipment in the big London stores – which tired me out, though I refused to admit it – we set off by train from Waterloo to Southampton. And now here we are in the inn at Ryde; the water sparkles, you can taste the salt in the breeze, and I feel that my whole life lies before me, and I'm happy, happier than I have been for months and months.

138

Carisbrooke Castle
August, 1883

Today I fulfilled a long-held ambition, and it was – strange to say, since we live in this imperfect world – every bit as nice as I'd thought it would be. But something else happened too, something terribly important and not wholly welcome . . . When I think of this day in years to come, which emotion will predominate? At all events, today was a day I will never forget.

How could a girl of fifteen years old have a long-held ambition? you might be thinking. How ridiculous! Well, my ambition was a simple one – to visit Carisbrooke Castle. That's all, and now I've done it.

I've told you before about my romantic passion for

Charles I, the martyred king. I allow that it must seem strange that I feel so strongly for a man long dead – and indeed, my own ancestor Edmund Ludlow signed his death warrant! I think it was Aunt Barbara who started my interest. She told me all about the king's men and the Parliamentarians, the Cavaliers and the Roundheads, and she showed me the pictures in the National Gallery – and who could help preferring the Cavaliers, with their rippling curls and beautiful lace collars, to the hard-eyed bull-faced Roundheads? Aunt Bar read me the poem Andrew Marvell wrote about the manner in which the king met his death, and it made me want to cry:

> He nothing common did or mean
> Upon that memorable scene,
> But with his keener eye
> The axe's edge did try;
> Nor called the Gods, with vulgar spite,
> To vindicate his helpless right,
> But bowed his comely head
> Down, as upon a bed.

Since then, Aunt Bar has explained, several times and in

her most earnest manner, that King Charles's belief in the Divine Right of Kings was mistaken, that Oliver Cromwell in many ways laid the foundations for our democratic system which, for all its faults, puts more power into the hand of the people than . . . but I'm afraid most of her words float over my head, and I lose myself in thoughts of how I would have comforted my hero as he stared death in the face, how I and I alone could have brought a glow into those mournful velvety eyes, which seemed to contain all the sorrows of the world.

When I first heard that our holiday was to be on the Isle of Wight, I skipped for joy, because I knew that Carisbrooke, where King Charles had been imprisoned, was on the island. How often had I entered that castle in my daydreams – dressed as a serving maid, I, a loyal nobleman's daughter, smuggled a prayer book and a crucifix and a nosegay of flowers into his cell; my hand resting lightly on his shoulder, I murmured messages of encouragement from his exiled children. And now I was to see the real Carisbrooke, to touch the very walls that had held my hero captive two and a half centuries ago! How much has changed in those centuries. This is still a royal island; our own dear Queen has her holiday home here, at Osborne House, and I believe she is very fond of it. The danger of execution must be far from her mind!

We drove there in a funny sort of open-topped coach. It was the jolliest drive. Little clouds scudded across the pale-blue sky like white rabbits, and despite our sun-bonnets, the breeze whipped tendrils of hair round our faces. This annoyed Mabel, who wanted to look her best for reasons which will later become apparent. We had left off our mourning clothes for the holiday because Aunt Nanny said it wasn't healthy to wear fusty old black when one is out of doors a good deal. Mabel revelled in her new pink peplum jacket, close-fitting with mother-of-pearl buttons and leg-of-mutton sleeves, and matching ribbons securing her bonnet, but the wind's attempts to rearrange her resulted in a most unbecoming scowl. I, however, enjoyed the feeling. After so long in the sickroom, sunshine and wind were very sweet to me.

The Island is such a picturesque, old-fashioned place. There are little glades, and glens, and waterfalls, and rocky outcrops, and the low-clipped hedgerows are tangled with honeysuckle and wild clematis. The labourers in the fields turned and stared at us as if they'd never seen a stranger in their lives; they tugged their forelocks in the most deferential manner! We came across a cluster of cottage girls playing hopscotch in the road; they threw us little bouquets of wildflowers, while their brothers turned somersaults for our entertainment, and we threw them our ha'pence in return.

The coach party consisted of myself and Mabel, Aunt Nanny (wearing her stern grey bonnet that makes her look like a general officer), Isa with her fan and her lacy parasol, and Emilie, their faithful French maid who accompanies them on all their travels, laden with rugs and shawls and medicaments and everything they could possibly need. You will notice that ours was an entirely female group. Our male escorts – Uncle Ben, with Bob at his heels, and Arthur Glover – were waiting for us outside the Red Lion at Carisbrooke where we were to lunch. Yes, true to his word Mr Glover has come over to the Island for a few days – exact length of time unspecified. This morning, Uncle Ben took him out sailing in a cutter. Mabel and I were forbidden to join them, on the flimsy grounds that we would be seasick. Hmmm. I wonder. It seems more likely to me that my uncle and Mabel's admirer had matters of state to discuss.

When Arthur Glover handed Mabel down from the coach,

I saw her raise her eyebrows a little, as if in question, and I saw her question answered by a smile and the slightest possible nod. I don't think anybody else saw. We all trooped into the garden of the inn, where a cold collation had been spread for us in the shade of some trees. I was so impatient to see the castle that I could hardly do justice to my luncheon, even though it included the most delicious crab patties. It seemed to me that Aunt Nanny took an inordinate amount of time over her meal. She sent back a chicken because, she said, it was insufficiently cooked, though the rest of us could detect nothing amiss.

At last all were ready to depart. My heart thumped as we walked up to the castle. The day had grown very warm; Isa, who is far from slender, became quite red in the face, and declared that when we got there she simply *must* sit in the shade. So Emilie set up a little camp with rugs and folding stools, and then she set about fanning Isa while Aunt Nanny got out her sketchbook. Nanny wanted me to sit and sketch with her, but I was reluctant. I was itching to explore the castle, and my aunt's strictures on the mistakes I was bound to make were more than I could bear.

Uncle Ben came to my rescue. 'You can't expect the child to sit still, Nan. Can't you see she's skittering about like a water wagtail?' It was decided that he should guide me round the castle – Uncle Ben always seems to know all about the places he visits, he's a very clever man – while Emilie should act as chaperone to Mabel and Mr Glover, who had expressed a desire to perambulate in the meadow below the castle walls. I was glad I did not have to dog their heels. I found their habit of rolling their eyes at one another somewhat irksome, and besides, Mabel has always been wont to tease me about my passion for King Charles.

Uncle Ben took me firmly by the hand, as if I had been a nervous child, and, with Bob panting close behind, he led me towards the well where the patient donkeys turned the waterwheel. The creak of the wheel, the soft trampling sound of the donkeys' hooves – would these have reached my king, through his barred window? Though well fed and well kept, these donkeys were just as much prisoners as he had been. Did such a thought pass through his mind?

We toured the building, the stone the same grey as the donkeys' coats. Uncle Ben pointed out the window through which the poor king had tried to escape, but had wedged himself fast. But it was in the chapel that I felt closest to his poor suffering spirit. I entered it alone – Uncle Ben stayed outside because of Bob, but I think he was glad of the excuse, because he dislikes churches and chapels. There were no other visitors. Revelling in my solitude, I knelt as close as I dared to the high altar, and raised my eyes to the richly ornamented coffered ceiling. And – I know it sounds fanciful – but it was as if I was touched by the wing tip of the Holy Spirit, just as I believe King Charles was touched, when the darkest hour came.

I rejoined Uncle Ben on the battlements. Bob had found a patch of shade, and was lolling there, his pink tongue dangling. I have to say that, now that he's a landlubber, Bob has become awfully fat! He was wearing a grand new collar, embroidered for him by a lady admirer. It read, 'R.I.P. *Eira*', in memory of Uncle Ben's ship. R.I.P., of course, means Rest In Peace. I suppose the poor old ship is peaceful, lying on the seabed.

Uncle Ben dared me to walk along the top of the battlements. When he lifted me up, the clasp of his strong hands filled me with the sense of safety mixed with adventure that I had always found in his touch, and I danced my way along the jagged walls. Red valerian spurted in profusion from the grey stones – red, I told myself, for the blood of the martyred king. I pulled out a tuft by its roots, and wrapped it in my handkerchief – later I soaked the handkerchief with water from the well. The valerian's in a tumbler now, here in my room at the inn. Tomorrow I shall pack its roots with damp moss, if I can find any. I shall take it back to Yotes with me and ask Weekes to plant it.

At last Uncle Ben recalled that I was supposed to be convalescing, and told me it was time to rest. He swept me off the wall, one hand over my mouth to silence my half-joking protests, and deposited me on a patch of close-mown turf in the spreading shade of a cedar tree. Bob ambled up, and provided me with a welcome, if over-warm, back rest! Uncle Ben stretched himself out beside us, propped up on one elbow.

I set about picking daisies to make a chain. I find my hands never want to be still – they must hold a pen or a paintbrush or pick flowers. 'Little Lilybel, you look as if you are making a bridal wreath,' said Uncle Ben.

The sound of the name by which Papa called me brought a rush of warmth to my face. I followed the direction of my uncle's gaze to the scene in the meadow below. Mabel was seated on one end of a bench. Arthur Glover knelt at her feet, gazing up adoringly at her face. The sun glinted on his crisp curls. Even at this distance, I could see that my sister's face was as pink as the ribbons on her sun-bonnet. At the other end of the bench sat Emilie, absorbed in her embroidery.

I must have frowned, for Uncle Ben said, 'I don't believe you like what you see any more than I do, little Lilybel. But Mabel believes herself to be mistress of her own destiny, and she no longer pays heed to my advice. If she believes that young Glover can save her from herself, so be it. The world is full of fools rushing into marriage like rats into a well-baited trap.'

I wondered what he meant by 'save her from herself', but I didn't ask, because I didn't want to hear the answer. I pursed my lips. 'I shall not be one of those fools, for I shall never marry.'

Uncle Ben laughed. 'You seem to have given your heart to the memory of poor hapless King Charles, so perhaps you never will. But if you change your mind, I trust you will not bestow yourself on so poor a creature as young Glover.'

I felt bold enough to ask questions, but just then we were joined by Aunt Nanny and Isa. '*There* you are!' exclaimed Nanny. 'We thought you were quite lost. Ben! I might have known it! The child is sitting on damp grass!'

'Hardly damp, Nan, on a sweltering August afternoon.'

'Nonsense! *I* know, and I beg to inform you, that on an island like this one the ground retains its moisture all summer long. If you want Milicent to catch rheumatic fever, this is the way to go about it.'

'Rheumatic fever? Nan, she's fifteen, not eighty-five.' But Uncle Ben knew he had lost. We rose to our feet, somewhat sheepishly, and the moment when I could have discovered why my uncle considered Mabel's choice such a poor one, was gone.

Arthur Glover saw us into our coach, then took his leave; our inn is full, so he has taken lodgings elsewhere. Aunt Nanny fussed about my health all the way back to Ryde. She has decreed that I must be carried upstairs, which is absurd when you consider how I was skipping along the castle battlements. But I knew that if I rebelled, Nan would find ingenious ways of prolonging my convalescence, so at her command I lay on the chaise longue in the inn's parlour, bereft of anything to read or write on, or even to sew. I closed my eyes and tried to recapture the thoughts I had had in the chapel. I thought about how I had really *felt*

for King Charles, and how this had struck me as the most important thing about being human, to be able somehow to touch the heart or the soul of another human being, even if only in one's imagination. And then Mabel came in.

She drew up a chair close to the chaise longue, and took my hand. I mistook her intense expression for one of anxiety, and said, 'I'm not a bit ill you know, it's just Aunt Nan –' and she said, 'I know, I know. But I have something to tell you.' She drew off her thin cotton gloves, and spread her left hand before my face. On the third finger, there glinted a ring; an opal held in a circle of tiny pearls.

I touched the opal, and Mabel twisted her hand so that I could see the flash of fire within it. I looked into her face, and couldn't think what to say. 'Little sister,' Mabel whispered. 'It's a chance for me. It's my best chance. Be happy for me, because I don't think anyone else is.'

The spirit that had moved me in the chapel moved me then, and I flung my arms round her. What did it matter what I, or Uncle Ben, or anyone else thought of Arthur Glover? Mabel had made her choice, and she deserved to find happiness.

We held each other close, as we had not done since the day Harry left for India. 'I know you will love him, when you truly know him,' she said, 'and of course, you will always have a home with us. Oh, Milicent, you have always been the best little sister to me.'

Opal for Tears
September, 1883

We spent a whole month on the Isle of Wight. My course
of warm salt-water baths, taken on the pier, must have
had the desired effect, or perhaps the shock of Mabel's
engagement distracted Aunt Nanny from the state of my
health – whatever the reason, it wasn't long before I was
allowed to do more or less as I pleased, as long as I submitted
to being carried upstairs to bed and to swallowing three of
her homeopathic pills each morning. I thoroughly enjoyed
bathing in the sea and scrambling on the cliffs; I even went
sailing with Uncle Ben, and no, I did *not* feel sick, though
others did!

Needless to say, Aunt Nanny was unable to keep her

opinions about Mr Glover to herself. Her campaign against him began as soon as Mabel put her engagement ring on public display. 'My dear, not an *opal*? Have you never heard the saying "an opal for tears"?'

Mabel had not. In vain she explained that the ring was a Glover family heirloom, last worn by Arthur's great-grandmother, or some such person. 'An heirloom, indeed!' snorted Aunt Nanny. 'Who are these Glovers, that they dare pride themselves on their heirlooms? I have heard nothing good of the Glovers.'

'And I am sure you have heard nothing bad, either!' retorted Mabel hotly. 'Arthur's family are entirely respectable. His father is a solicitor in the City, and they keep a brougham and a Victoria!'

'That,' said our aunt, 'means little. The surname alone tells one all one needs to know. A glover – one who makes gloves.'

I thought that making gloves was a rather ingenious thing to do, and besides, I doubted that any member of Arthur's family had made a glove since the Middle Ages, but I kept my thoughts to myself. Mabel, unwisely, pointed out that our aunt's own surname was only Smith, albeit distinguished by the prefix 'Leigh'.

Aunt Nanny rose to her full, considerable, height. 'I have the greatest possible prejudice against the Glovers, for reasons I can no longer remember,' she declared, icily. And, gathering her rustling skirts in one hand, she swept out of the room.

Despite her anger, Mabel could not help smiling at the absurdity of Aunt Nanny's objections. Isa, ever the peacemaker, took up Mabel's ring hand and stroked it. 'Dear Mappy,' she said – Isa often used the pet names we had gone by when we were children – 'You must remember that neither Nan nor your Uncle Ben set great store by marriage. I sometimes think they would be happier if nobody ever married at all. But for what *my* opinion is worth, I think it is a very pretty ring.'

'Oh, Isa, you know your opinion is worth a great deal!' And Mabel leaned forward to place a kiss on Isa's plump cheek.

For several days, Aunt Nanny expounded on the unsatisfactory attributes of the Glover family – which were, in summary, that they were not rich enough, not educated enough, and they gave themselves airs and graces. When Arthur himself came to call, she received him with a kind of exaggerated but chilly politeness. But after a while she changed tack. There was one unlucky picnic expedition to Blackgang Chine when my future brother-in-law was seized with a fit of coughing and sneezing. He protested that it was only sitting in the long grass that had brought it on, but Nanny dismissed this theory. She detected a constitutional weakness. Looking at Arthur's ruddy complexion and broad-shouldered frame it was not possible, for me at any rate, to imagine any lurking disease, but our aunt has made a lifelong study of the ill health of others, and she made haste to share her anxieties with Mabel. As soon as Arthur had returned to his own lodging for the night, she waded in. 'My dear, it is a serious undertaking – to marry a man who may provide you with nothing but a troop of wretched, sickly children.'

Mabel let out an unladylike shout of derisive laughter, and Isa murmured, 'Dear Nan, that is a *little* unfair.' But Nanny had the bit between her teeth, and throughout our last week on the Island she regaled us with many a tale of young women of her acquaintance who had found themselves saddled with useless, invalid husbands.

Uncle Ben was just as bad. He stated publically what he had already told me privately – that since Mabel was 'of age' he could not prevent the marriage, much though he wished he could. 'I am glad you are not my daughter,' he told Mabel when she tried to remonstrate with him, and, though I love my uncle almost more than anyone else in the world, I thought that was less than kind. Indeed, the hostile attitude of the older generation made me look more favourably on poor Mr Glover than I ever had before. After all, he had not – as yet – done any of us any harm.

Uncle Ben's objections were twofold. Firstly, he said that Mr Glover was more interested in Mabel's money than in Mabel herself. Secondly, he thought it very poor show that, as yet, the young man had not gone in for any profession, or made any attempt to make his way in the world. This surprised and worried me too. How could a young man have no ambition when the world was at his feet? How often had I longed to be a boy, so that I could lead a life of purpose and adventure! I could have been a soldier, like my father, or a physician, like Dr Moore, or an explorer, like Uncle Ben, or even a farmer, like Uncle Willy. Oh to be a boy and to have the freedom to choose!

When I was enduring one of my aunt-enforced 'rests' on the chaise longue, Isa came and sat beside me, and gave in to my often-repeated request that she should read my fortune in my palm. She has a little knowledge of such arts, though she always begs people not to take her words seriously. But Mabel's impending marriage had made me even more curious about my own future, and at last my nagging prevailed.

Isa took my thin brown hand between her two chubby pale ones and examined it. She ran a fingertip along the lines that dissected my palm like bolts of lightning, and asked me to curl my fingers over so that she could count the creases that formed just below my little finger. 'I see a long life,' she said at last, 'a long life, but not always an easy one. There are obstacles to be overcome. But they *will* be overcome, because there is a core of great strength.'

So far I had confided my ambition to no one other than Aunt Barbara, so I felt shy when I asked, 'Can you see any sign that I might become a writer, or anything of that nature?'

Isa held my hand closer to her eyes. 'The marks of creativity are faint, but they are not absent. It is possible, though not certain. But then, nothing is certain. Fortune-telling can only indicate what is more *likely* to happen; no one can truly predict the future.'

'Except God.'

'Except God. And He will not reveal our futures to

us, for then we would not have to think for ourselves. He bestows on us certain gifts, and places opportunities within our reach, but it is for us to decide how to make use of them.'

I sensed that Isa had not told me of everything she had seen in my hand, and I felt myself blush as I broke the little silence that had arisen between us. 'Isa – will I ever – can you see signs that I might –'

She caught my meaning, and laughed. 'Dearest Lilybel, you would be a most unusual girl if you did not want to know about marriage and children! So don't be shy, I will tell you what I see. But I think you *are* unusual, because your hand gives a hazy reading on this subject. Most hands state these facts quite clearly, but yours – I am not sure. These little creases here – they indicate the number of children, which would seem to be three, but they are so indistinct that it is possible there will be none. And this mark here may mean a husband, but he seems to be a long way off.'

'I'm glad. I think I would rather have him a long way off.'

Isa patted my arm. 'I expect our lack of enthusiasm for poor Mabel's news has not exactly encouraged thoughts of matrimony in you. But keep an open mind on the subject, my dear. Though the glamour of an engagement soon wears off, nothing can match the deep joy that comes from joining lives with your Own Particular One. I know, for I have found that joy.'

It startled me, just a little, to realise that Isa was talking, not about a husband, but about Aunt Nanny. I smiled feebly, and said, 'That must be very nice,' because it would have been rude to say nothing.

'It must seem harsh to you,' Isa went on, 'to hear Nan and Ben disparaging Mr Glover, and indeed I think they go too far. But, my dear, remember they are concerned above all for Mabel's future happiness, and they are not convinced that Mr Glover can guarantee it.'

'I must admit,' I replied, 'that I would rather Mabel married a man with more gumption. But I take comfort in the knowledge that he is a friend of Harry's, and I don't agree with Uncle Ben, that he only cares about Mabel's money.'

'I think you are right. The young couple take great pleasure in each other's company. I could wish that Mabel had made the acquaintance of a wider range of young men, before making up her mind . . . but, as you say, Harry's approval counts for a great deal. Dear Harry, how good it will be when he returns from India safe and sound!'

I missed Isa when she and Aunt Nanny returned to Algiers, once they had seen us settled back at Yotes Court. It was good to talk to someone who was both in our family and yet not truly of it; dear, kind Isa is free of that habit of criticism that makes so many of my relations rather challenging companions. I even missed Aunt Nanny, in a way, for she is never dull. Mabel, however, did not. 'Thank Heavens for that!' she exclaimed, when we had waved them off at the station. 'I really could not have *borne* to have Aunt Nanny making all my wedding plans for me.'

It was lovely to get back to Yotes, to be welcomed by our dear servants, not to mention the dogs and horses! Almost the first thing I did was to go to the stables to reacquaint myself with Robin Hood. I had not ridden him since June, before I caught diphtheria. I leaned my head against his sleek black neck and breathed in his warm smell and fondled his velvet nose, and murmured my apology to him, and he snickered his acceptance and promised me many adventures, or so I liked to imagine.

On the face of it, life hasn't changed. Every morning Evelyn Stapleton and I go to our lessons in the schoolroom, and in the afternoons we ride or walk or run errands for Creathy. With Aunt Nanny gone, no one suspects me of being an invalid any more, so I can enjoy September to the full. I love this time of year – the diamond dew drops on the grass in the early morning, the fruit-pickers' ladders resting against the orchard trees, the baskets full of plums and early apples nestling in the long wet grass. Most of all, I love hop picking. Mabel and I have been down to help pick, as we always do – Papa let us do that, as long as we were escorted, and now Mr Glover escorts us, so I suppose he has his uses.

He hasn't done any picking himself, men rarely do, because it requires nimble fingers. It's hot, dirty work; we come back with stained hands and scraps of leaf in our disordered hair and rents in our aprons, and Creathy clucks her tongue, but I love the warm, yeasty smell of the hops and the satisfaction of seeing the bins fill up with cleanly picked flowers – no leaves or bits of vine are allowed. And I love the songs and jokes of the other pickers. While the women and children pick, the men do the heavy work, collecting the full bins and taking them off to be weighed, then dried in the oast houses. Some of them are gypsies, some are Irish travellers, some are the families of our regular farm labourers here at Mereworth. Creathy says their conversation is not suitable for the ears of young ladies, but I airily assure her that I don't understand much of it, and indeed I don't!

Arthur – I am getting used to calling him by his Christian name – rides over to Yotes nearly every day. He seems to play an ever larger part in the running of the house, and I suppose he has a right to do so. The plans for their life after the wedding remain unclear. Some days they talk as if they mean to set up home together at Yotes, but sometimes they speculate about farming in Argentina, or New Zealand. I can't see Mabel as a farmer's wife, somehow, though I suppose she might enjoy running a large estate. But to be so far away from home! The voyage to New Zealand takes, I believe, six weeks. Would I go with them? It would certainly be an adventure . . . But what would happen to Yotes? Could it be that this is the last year I will ever take part in the picking of the hops?

But perhaps we will stay here, after all. As I write, my brother-in-law-to-be is outside, digging a ditch near the watercress beds. He and Mabel are both longing for the hunting season to begin; the ditch is for jumping practice. They spend as much time on horseback as is humanly possible. When it rains, they sit indoors and paint. Arthur is painting a coat-of-arms for Mabel, who seems to talk about ancestry rather a lot these days, and she is painting a portrait of him, in oils. The colours are somewhat lurid, and make him look like a prize fighter, and one who has let his opponent get the better of him at that! When they are tired of painting they snuggle up together on the piano stool and sing sentimental duets.

I'm not a good audience, I'm afraid. When they start their warbling, I tend to find a pressing engagement elsewhere – I need to finish my German composition, or see to the hampers, or help Creathy label the new pots of jam. Not that the happy pair notice my slipping away. They gaze so long into each other's eyes that they observe little else. Marriage is called 'wedlock', and certainly they seem locked together. That's not a state that would suit me.

I like it better when there are guests in the house. Mabel likes crowds, and her engagement has made little difference to that. Last Saturday, she invited a troop of friends and neighbours to come and play cricket, but when, as Creathy put it, it 'rained cats and dogs', instead of cancelling the party Mabel decreed that we should play cricket in the attic! The attic passage runs the whole length of the house. We propped up broken chairs at either end for wickets, and had *great* fun. Harry would have adored it. His bowling is quite famous.

When we were all exhausted, we took refreshment in the drawing room, and somebody suggested we play charades. You separate into teams; each team chooses a word, divides it into syllables, acts out each syllable, and finally acts out the whole word, and the other teams have to guess it. Evelyn Stapleton and I found ourselves in the same team as Arthur and Mabel. The word we chose was 'matrimony' – *quelle surprise!* – which we divided into 'mat', 'tree', 'moan' and 'knee'. For 'tree', we got up a scene of Charles II – the son of my hero, of course – hiding in an oak tree while Cromwell's men searched for him in vain. I was Charles – lucky me – and what do you think we used for the oak tree? Arthur himself! We wrapped him in brownish sacking, and then he had to stand as still and firm as he could while I clambered onto his shoulders and 'hid' under a green silk parasol! *Not* very dignified. I have to say, he played his part to perfection.

'Tree' did not provide much opportunity for a romantic display, but when it came to 'knee', Arthur went down on bended knee and made a great show of begging for Mabel's hand. Not very subtle, and I'm sure most of the audience had guessed our word long before the end. But the rule of the game is that no guesses are to be made before the play is played out, so the amorous couple had the delight of enacting the whole word, 'matrimony'. Funnily enough, they chose to mime a quarrelsome couple at a mock breakfast-time, bickering over the teacups, with much sighing and shrugging of shoulders, while Evelyn and I pretended to be their two little children, squabbling on the floor over possession of my old doll, and tugging at each others' hair.

The word was, indeed, easily guessed, amid much laughter. Everyone was so jolly, no one seemed inclined to go home. Evelyn – bold girl – suggested that we try 'mesmerism'. And she the daughter of a clergyman too! This is how mesmerism works: by chanting and repeating certain phrases, a person can be put into a trance, and become suggestible and almost weightless, and can be lifted by the merest touch of fingertips. I was chosen as the victim – I'm not sure that's the right word – quite possibly because I was the lightest person in the room. Mabel gave orders to the servants that we were on no account to be interrupted until she rang the bell. Then the shutters were closed, the candles extinguished; the only light in the room was the flickering fire.

I was bidden to remove my shoes, and untie my hair. I wondered what kind of a little moppet I looked, as I stood there in my stockinged feet, with my wispy hair straggling over my shoulders. First the company joined hands, and marched round and round me chanting my name until I felt quite giddy. Then when Evelyn said, 'Down!' I lay on the floor. The furniture had been pushed back, and I lay in the middle of the room, under the unlit chandelier, which tinkled softly because of the tramping footsteps, and glinted like rubies in the firelight. The others knelt in a circle round me. They placed the tips of their first two fingers just underneath my body – lightly, so that I felt no pressure. Then a chant began and passed round the circle from mouth to mouth: 'She looks pale – she looks pale – she looks pale.'

At last this changed to, 'She looks ill – she looks ill.' A poem came into my head, a poem written by a friend of Aunt Barbara's, about Irish fairies, and how they stole away a human child:

> They stole little Bridget
> For seven years long;
> When she came down again
> Her friends were all gone.
> They took her lightly back,
> Between the night and morrow,
> They thought that she was fast asleep,
> But she was dead with sorrow.
> They have kept her ever since
> Deep within the lake,
> On a bed of flag-leaves,
> Watching till she wake.

I saw myself as little Bridget, in a long white gown, lying 'deep within the lake' with my hair spread out behind me and my hands crossed at my breast. And I felt, not frightened, but peaceful; sorrowful, yes, but as if I were a vessel full of sorrow, just so much and no more. Strange to say, I felt as if in that moment I understood death more clearly than when I had lain, in danger, on my bed of sickness.

The chant changed. 'She is dying – she is dying – she is dying,' murmured the voices like the wind in the reeds. I knew that when they reached 'she is dead', they would lift me with the faintest touch of their fingertips, and my weightless body would rise into the air. And I truly felt as if this would happen.

But I never found out, because just at the crucial moment, Mabel jumped up, and rang the bell for the servants long and loud. There were some disappointed groans from the others, and some protests, but Arthur flung open the shutters and placed his arm, briefly but tenderly, round Mabel's shoulders. I sat up on my elbows, blinking. My sister's face was contorted by a look of horror. I have seen that look before, somewhere, long, long ago.

'Mabel is right to call a halt,' said Arthur. 'General Ludlow would not have wanted us to continue.' His tone was firm and manly. I felt most peculiar, as if I had been hauled up out of deep, deep water, but even in my dazed condition I felt a new respect for him.

Then there was Louisa at the door, and Mabel giving her orders to bring tea and sandwiches, and the stir of some people making their departures, and Evelyn, irrepressible, organising those remaining in a game of 'vingt-et-un', with our little mother-of-pearl counters shaped like fish as the stakes. I laced up my shoes, tied back my hair, and joined in the game as if nothing had happened at all.

The Sycamore Leaf
October, 1883

My farewell to my childhood home may have happened already, and I was in too much of a rush to take it in! Poor old Yotes.

We were alone for once, Mabel and I, when we received the news that would change our lives for ever. It was a perfect September evening. We wrapped shawls round our shoulders and strolled out into the park. A full moon, fuzzy edged, apricot coloured, hung above the avenue of twisted chestnuts. All we could hear was a faint whine from the spirals of gnats above the lake, the occasional splash as a fish broke the surface, the distant calling of owls, and the noise like tearing silk that the horses made as their strong teeth cropped the grass in the paddock that borders the lawn.

We were talking of Harry's return. His ship was expected any day. A thin lilac cloud drifted across the face of the moon like a gauzy scarf. Was our brother admiring the moon at this very moment, as it paved a glittering road across the sea? Harry's letters from India had complained of the heat. How delightful that he would return to this glorious English autumn! Before us lay the sleeping park; behind, the comfortable solidity of the old house, its windows glowing a welcome. If I had known, I would have chosen that perfect moment to bid it farewell.

A four-wheeler, driven faster than usual, was coming down the avenue. We heard it before we saw it. 'Are we expecting anyone?' I asked. Mabel frowned. 'No, nobody. Unless Arthur –' But Arthur always arrived on horseback.

The horses were reined in sharply in front of the house; gravel sprayed up from their hooves. The carriage door opened and out bounded Bob. He dashed towards us with a frenzy of excited barks, but our cries of delighted welcome died in our throats when we looked up and saw Uncle Ben, hatless, his shoulders stooped. How did I know, in that instant, that it was Harry who was dead?

Uncle Ben gave us the plain facts, simply and quickly. Harry had died of a fever, on board ship, somewhere in the Red Sea. Arrangements had already been made. His body would be returned to us for burial; his belongings would arrive separately. Uncle Ben folded us both in his arms. We felt, rather than heard, the sob that shook his body.

Mabel and I could find no words as he led us back to the house. Creathy met us at the door. She had already begun her preparations for bed, but the unexpected sound of the carriage had brought her back downstairs. There she stood in her woolly brown wrapper, her thin grey plait hanging down her back, as solid and familiar as the house itself. Something inside me gave way. 'Oh, Creathy, Harry's dead!' I cried, and fell into her arms in a storm of weeping.

We unpacked Harry's things together, Mabel, Creathy and I. We wouldn't let the servants help. When the trunks were opened, out drifted a strange, spicy, exotic smell, which made me feel that we were opening a tomb.

We hung everything in his wardrobe, just as if he would be needing it again in a few days' time. It didn't occur to us to do anything else. One box contained souvenirs from

India, surely intended as gifts for us. There were shawls from Kashmir, richly coloured, and so fine that they could be drawn through Mabel's engagement ring. There were carved sandalwood boxes – it was these that gave off the spicy smell. An intricately wrought silver necklace, set with tiger's-eye stone – which of us was this meant for? A baby camel's skin, smooth, almost silky. Bronze bells suspended from a strip of leather, like a rein – Mabel suggested that they must have formed part of an elephant's harness. A fan, cleverly constructed from the eye part of peacock's feathers, closely overlapping. And more. And more. We piled it all on the bed and left it there, defeated by sorrow.

Uncle Ben took charge of the funeral arrangements. Harry was, of course, to be buried in the family grave, with Mama, Papa and Edmund, the brother I never knew. I couldn't get the idea out of my head that when the grave was opened, I would see the three of them lying there, even though I knew perfectly well that they were tightly sealed in their coffins.

In the church we sang 'Lead, Kindly Light' and 'Abide With Me', and Mabel's voice rang out clear and true, without a tremor. But when it came to the burial . . .

We stood in a circle round the grave, in the darkest

corner of the churchyard, where a yew tree spreads its shaggy branches so far that little can grow beneath it. I've been told that the yew is very old, older even than William the Conqueror's victory over Harold in 1066. I have found that comforting, to think that my family lie in the embrace of something so ancient and yet still living.

'Man that is born of woman, hath but a short time to live, and is full of misery; he cometh up and is cut down like a flower.' Mr Stapleton's words tolled in my ears like a church bell. I stole glimpses at the faces of my family as they watched the coffin being lowered into the ground. Uncle Ben's strong features looked as if they had been carved out of granite; he could have been a statue of a ruler of the ancient world. But Aunt Barbara's face was dissolving. Her flesh seemed soft and loose, and she made no attempt to check her tears. She made me think of a river, rushing ever onwards towards its dissolution in the sea. Aunt Jenny, the white oval of her face framed by black drapery, looked more than ever like a beautiful skull. Mabel stood beside me. I didn't dare look at her.

I could see the tiny coffin of my brother Edmund; its embroidered linen covering looked as clean and fresh as if it had been placed there that very day. The wreath of sweet-smelling white gardenias from our hothouse that had dignified Harry's coffin was laid to one side on the grass. Mabel had made it, under instruction from Aunt Barbara. I desperately wanted to save a scrap of it, a single bloom and a couple of leaves.

'In the midst of life we are in death.' How forcefully the fifteen years of my own life had borne out the words of the Prayer Book! Down went the coffin. What a work of labour it is, to dispose of a human body! In one of his letters, Harry had told me that some Indians – Parsees, I think – leave their dead on top of a stone tower, to have their bones picked clean by vultures. I think I would prefer that to the mossy dankness of the tomb.

'Earth to earth, ashes to ashes, dust to dust.' We each hold a posy, Aunt Bar, Mabel and I, to throw in with the coffin as a farewell to Harry. Aunt Bar's was made of rosemary, for remembrance. Mine was made of sprigs from the bushes that grew round our stables. I had bound the stalks with hairs combed from the tails of each of our horses. I hadn't told anyone that.

Aunt Bar, supported by her kind maid Henrietta, tossed hers in with a ringing cry of 'adieu'. I pressed mine to my lips, and whispered, 'Goodbye, my brother.' But Mabel's posy fell from her fingers as she sank to the ground in a swoon.

❧ ❧ ❧

I wish I could tell you that that was the worst of it, but there was more to come. Here I am at Crowham, curled in the wicker rocking chair on the veranda, lulled by the drowsy drone of bluebottles and the chirrups and scratchings of Bully, Roddy's pet bullfinch, as he clambers round his cage clinging to the bars, and scatters his seed on the floor below. Floss, Aunt Jenny's fluffy tortoiseshell cat, is nursing her three new kittens in a basket in the corner. I can see them, blindly kneading her warm side with their flat little paws. Though October has just begun, the air is mild and still, and the veranda is flooded with golden light. I rock, slowly, and don't even attempt to get on with the knitting – a tam-o'-shanter for little Dolly – that lies in my lap. Cook, who thinks I am wasting away, brought me a mug of sweet cocoa and some of the thick, buttery, crumbly biscuits that are her speciality, so I'm feeling full and heavy. Those biscuits have always been such a feature of our visits to Crowham. Harry particularly liked them. I am struggling to make myself realise that he won't ever taste them again.

This is the first moment I've had to myself since whatever happened, happened. I've been putting off writing about it, but I'll work up to it now. Aunt Jenny and Uncle Willy took me back with them to Crowham straight afterwards. I don't mean straight after the funeral, I mean . . . after what I'm going to tell you about. We left in such a rush, I only had time to pack a few things, so I'm borrowing what I need from Roddy, who is a good deal taller than me but just as thin. Creathy will come on with all the luggage as soon as she can, but just now she can't leave Mabel. I'm going to have to tell you why.

It feels so strange to be here, in this sleepy old house nestling in its hollow. Nothing ever changes at Crowham, and yet, for me, everything has changed. I think Aunt Jenny has told her children that they mustn't leave me on my own, but Roddy, poor dear, is hardly enlivening company. She cries at least as much as I do. She was the closest cousin in age to Harry – only a year younger – and she feels it dreadfully. So does Willyboy, though, being male, he's not supposed to cry, not in public at least. He gives vent to his feeling by aiming cricket balls as hard as he can at the garden wall. He and Harry were always such good friends.

Lionel is a hard-hearted nine year old; he doesn't

understand why there's so much fuss, and that's actually a good thing. It's quite refreshing to have him drag me outside to bowl for him, though he complains that my underarm bowling isn't fast enough. I agree; overarm is much more powerful. If only we girls did not have to wear these silly, tight sleeves that make it impossible for us to raise our arms above our heads! When I'm grown up – which is not so very long now – I shall design my own clothes, as Aunt Bar does, so that I can move my body any way I please. Isn't it odd, how even when one is in the depths of sorrow one can still have thoughts about things like clothes and cricket?

Bella is too young to understand, though she gets very concerned if she sees one of us crying, and wipes our faces with her own little handkerchief, which isn't always spotlessly clean, for she uses it to wrap up the muddy treasures she finds in the garden. Dolly isn't even two; she just toddles over and climbs into our laps and pats our faces with her golden head on one side, as if she is offering sympathy even though she doesn't know why. But a moment later she wants to be bounced up and down, playing 'This Is the Way the Ladies Ride'. Sometimes Martha, their nurse, tries to hush them or shoo them away, but their funny little ways push sorrow to one side for a time, and that's welcome, because sorrow is exhausting.

They are darlings, but I am glad to have a moment to myself right now. Martha has taken the little girls, and a reluctant Lionel, for a walk, Dolly sitting up like a queen in the big perambulator that used to be mine. Aunt Jenny has taken Roddy into Hastings in the wagonette, to kit them both out in black cashmere. Uncle Willy is out shooting on the marsh, and Willyboy has gone too. Willyboy is an excellent shot. He and Harry used to shoot crows and pigeons together . . . but I must not allow myself to dwell on such memories. I need to tell you about Mabel, and in spite of the sunlight and the comfort and the warmth of the cocoa and biscuits inside me, that's what I will do.

When Mabel fell into a faint by the side of the grave, Arthur Glover, who was one of the pall-bearers, hurried over, and gathered her in his arms, and the anxiety and tenderness in his face made me regret that I'd ever thought him a shallow man. He loved Mabel, that was plain for all to see. But as soon as she came to, she tried to push him away. 'No, no,' she kept saying, 'I cannot see you, Arthur. You must keep away. You cannot save me. Please understand.'

Uncle Ben and Creathy persuaded him to let her go. They took Mabel back to Yotes in the carriage, leaving Arthur empty handed and alone.

We all stood about in the graveyard, bewildered. I held Aunt Bar's trembling hand. 'Try not to worry about Mabel, my elf-child,' she whispered. 'She is very unhappy, but she has a good deal of your father in her, and I think she will be all right in the end.'

Back at Yotes, everyone gathered for food and drink, but Mabel did not appear. Creathy at last came into the drawing room with a report; Mabel was quiet, and resting; Dr Hooker had given her a composing draught. It was better, said Creathy firmly, for her to have no visitors. Arthur Glover hissed in my ear, 'I *must* see her. I cannot leave until I have seen her.' He slipped from the room.

He must have gone to her bedchamber unaccompanied, which a gentleman would not ordinarily do, but I could see he felt that this was an emergency. And very soon the emergency turned into a disaster. The company in the drawing room were conversing in low, subdued voices, nibbling small sandwiches and sipping tea or sherry wine. People talked of horses, dogs, the harvest and the weather – anything but the subjects that were filling all our minds.

But then we all froze as a cry, a banshee wail, rent the air. I looked at Aunt Bar, and I heard her whisper, 'Bella – my poor sister'.

I ran from the room. Uncle Ben was just behind me. Mabel and Arthur Glover stood on the first-floor landing; he held her by the wrists. Her loose hair streamed over her shoulders, her clothing seemed awry, and her contorted face was almost unrecognisable. His voice, low and urgent, was trying to soothe her, but she was beyond soothing. 'I carry the family taint. Arthur, if I marry you, I will destroy you,' came her despairing cry, and with one lithe movement, slippery as an eel, she twisted out of his grasp and flung herself over the banisters.

With a great roar, Uncle Ben bounded across the floor to where she lay, a black crumpled heap like an injured blackbird on the cold stone floor. She had fallen just in front of the portrait of the lady in the pale-green dress, the one with the damaged face. In that instant I understood fully what I had always half known; that it was my mother who had damaged that portrait, just as she had tried to damage herself, and I understood what Aunt Bar had meant when she mouthed my mother's name.

Uncle Ben was pushing Mabel's hair away, trying to

see whether her head was injured. One arm was folded awkwardly beneath her; I could see that that, at least, was broken. Uncle Ben held the palms of his hand in front of her mouth, to feel her breath upon it. 'She's alive,' he said. 'She's got a chance.'

Aunt Jenny bundled me away from Yotes before I could ascertain the full extent of Mabel's injuries, but a telegram arrived from Uncle Ben not long after we reached Crowham: 'Arm broken ribs cracked bruising face unharmed state of mind uncertain Ben.' When Roddy and I repaired to bed that night we kneeled down together and thanked the Lord for Mabel's life, but I wonder if Roddy thought, as I did, that her mind would take longer to heal than her arm and ribs.

Now here I am, packing up my belongings only a short while after Creathy had brought them to me at Crowham. It's all been decided. Mabel is at Gower Street with Uncle Ben, and I am to go to boarding school. Fifteen and a half, and off to school for the first time in my life! I'm actually quite excited.

Yotes has been shut up. Miss Kahn has returned to her

family in Germany, since it is deemed I no longer have need of her. She has promised to write very often. Perhaps I will be allowed to visit her some day.

Creathy will see me off to school, and then she will return to Gower Street. She has promised, and Uncle Ben has promised too, that she will not leave us. I am assured that I will always find her either at Gower Street or at Crowham. But for the time being, I am not to visit Gower Street. Nobody is to see Mabel, except Uncle Ben, Creathy, and the doctor. Arthur Glover, I am told, brings flowers to the door every day. I wonder if he catches a glimpse of her looking out from behind the curtains of the house that, just for now, has become her prison. The doctor has ordered that nothing must disturb her; she may not even receive letters. I hope Bob brings her comfort. I hope she can curl up on the polar-bear skin rug and lean against his woolly side.

The other thing I hope, is that kind Dr Moore will be allowed to treat Mabel. I know Uncle Ben doesn't like him, and he didn't approve of his marrying Amy. But even though Uncle Ben is my hero, I think he can be wrong about some things, and I am sure he is wrong about Dr Moore. I feel that Mabel needs a doctor who can treat her heart and mind as well as her body, who can see that the three are all closely bound up together. I think that Dr Moore would be able to make her see that, though Fate has dealt her a certain hand of cards, the way she plays them is up to her.

My boarding school is at Tunbridge Wells, so it is close to the places I know and love best, and my friends from Mereworth have promised to visit me. The best news of all is that Evelyn is to join me at the school! Mr and Mrs Stapleton have declared that Evelyn is 'bursting out of her bounds' at home, and that they regard the discipline of boarding school as the last chance to turn her into a respectable young lady! 'Not much chance of that,' she wrote in her last letter to me, 'but I say, Milicent, won't we have some larks!'

So here I am, with my clothes folded ready for packing in the room I've been sharing with Roddy, and Aunt Jenny is ticking things off on the list of necessaries the school has sent, and working out whether we'll need to make a last expedition to Hastings or whether I can make do with what I've got. And while Aunt Jenny's back is turned I'm slipping something into my tortoiseshell box of treasures. It's a sycamore leaf, still green, though stiffening with the onset of autumn; it has a hole cut into it, and the sides have been folded and twisted to make an inelegant kind of ring. What kind of treasure is this, you may well ask? Well, yesterday afternoon Willyboy and I found ourselves alone in the garden. We sat on the bench beneath the sycamore. For a while Willyboy scuffled at the gravel with the toe of his boot without saying much, then he sprang up and picked up a new-fallen leaf, and began to twist and tear it. 'M-M-Milicent,' he stammered, 'Do you e-e-ever think, that y-y-you and me, we-we-we're two of a kind?'

I looked into his earnest eyes, that are rather like a spaniel's, and suddenly I felt most awfully fond of him, and as though I didn't want to go away from Crowham. 'I think I know what you mean,' I said.

'I d-d-don't suppose I'll ever m-m-marry anyone,' he continued, twisting the leaf, 'B-b-but if there ever comes a time wh-when it's j-j-just you and m-m-me left, old girl, do you think we m-m-might marry each other?'

'I don't suppose I'll marry anyone, either,' I replied. 'But if, as you say, there's only we two left – well, it might be rather comfortable.' And we both laughed, and he took my hand and put the leaf-ring on my finger. 'P-p-please accept this token of my h-h-humble esteem,' he said, still with a little laugh in his voice, 'because there's n-no one that compares to you.'

At that moment the gong sounded for tea, and I slipped the leaf-ring into my pocket. I don't suppose I ever will marry dear old Willyboy, but I will keep the ring in my tortoiseshell box, because it is something to be thought incomparable, even once in a lifetime.

And now my packing is nearly done. Aunt Jenny has decided that my hair should be properly cut before I leave, and besides, it seems I need new pocket handkerchiefs. So we will set off for Hastings, she and I, in the wagonette, and then I will be ready to start my new life. But first I will seal up this journal, with black satin ribbon and black sealing wax, and lock it in my tortoiseshell box. And thus I, Milicent Bella Ludlow, motherless, fatherless, brotherless and all but sisterless, lay down my pen, bid farewell to my future self, and set off on my journey into the great unknown.

Author's Note

Milicent's Book is a true story. All the characters in it were real people, and most of the events in it really did take place.

I found out the story because I live in the house that Milicent bought when she was twenty years old. It's a big old house called Hancox, and it's full of family letters, sketchbooks and photographs. I found Milicent's tortoiseshell box of treasures, and two diaries that she kept when she was a teenager at Yotes Court. For *Milicent's Book*, I ran the events of two years into less than a single year, but apart from that I changed very little of her story. This is what happened next:

Mabel took a long time to recover from her breakdown. Her engagement to Arthur Glover was broken off; she lived by turns with Uncle Ben, Aunt Barbara and Uncle Willy and Aunt Jenny. Once she was well enough, and once Milicent had left school, the two sisters looked for a home together. They found Hancox, in East Sussex, close to many of their relatives. There was plenty of room for Mabel's horses, and Milicent had the walled kitchen garden she always wanted. To everyone's surprise, Milicent decided to manage the farm at Hancox herself. There can't have been many Victorian girls running their own farm, but Milicent was always unusual.

Creathy came to live with them too. Mabel became engaged again, this time to a second cousin with the peculiar name of Ludlow Coape Ludlow. Ludlow was a soldier; after the wedding he and Mabel went off to India to join his regiment. Creathy kept Milicent company after Mabel's departure.

Milicent divided her time between farming at Hancox and working with poor girls in the East End of London, teaching them and helping them to find jobs. Mabel and Ludlow returned from India, moved back into Hancox, and had three girls and a boy. They named their eldest daughter Eira, after Uncle Ben's ship. Little Eira's godmothers were Milicent and Florence Nightingale.

Milicent spent a lot of time with her cousin, the beautiful Amy, and her husband the kind Dr Moore. Amy needed help with her three children, Alan, Ethne (pronounced Enna) and Gillachrist, because she was very ill with tuberculosis. Milicent took Amy to Rome for the winter, hoping that a warmer climate would cure her disease, but Amy was very thin and weak, and she died.

Milicent helped Dr Moore a great deal with his motherless children, so it is not surprising that two years after Amy's death, she and Dr Moore got married. She was thirty-five and he was fifty-four, so I expect they decided they were too old to have children. Though Milicent never had her own baby, she was a busy stepmother and aunt.

Eventually, Milicent passed Hancox on to her stepson Alan, who was my grandfather. Alan didn't like throwing things away, which is why I have so much information about Milicent and her family. Alan kept many of her possessions. Milicent always stayed in touch with her relations, and she was friends with Nellie Stapleton her whole life long.

I imagine that Milicent would not be pleased with me for reading her diaries, but I hope that she would be glad to know that I and my three sons still live in her old home. If she could see it now, she would find that very little has changed since her time!

C. F. WING,   TUNBRIDGE WELLS.

Milicent, aged twelve

Milicent, aged fifteen

Milicent being presented at court, aged twenty-one